JESSICA BECK
THE DONUT MYSTERIES, BOOK 52
THE HOLE TRUTH

D1522637

Donut Mystery 52 The Hole Truth
Copyright © 2021 by Jessica Beck
All rights reserved
First edition: 2021

The First Time Ever Published!
The 52nd Donut Mystery

Jessica Beck is the *New York Times* Bestselling Author of the Donut Mysteries, the Cast Iron Cooking Mysteries, the Classic Diner Mysteries, and the Ghost Cat Cozy Mysteries.

WHEN RICHARD COVINGTON is murdered, his past leads Suzanne and her stepfather, Phillip, on a wild ride to the present as they search for the man's killer. To make matters worse, one of Suzanne's best friends is one of their main suspects, and Suzanne must walk the fine line between friendship and her compulsion to discover The Hole Truth.

As always,
To P and E,
And to Luna,
A fun, energetic, and loving spirit.
You will be missed dearly by those of us who loved you deeply,
And you will live forever in our hearts.

Chapter 1

"SUZANNE, I NEED YOU to sign these papers right now," Geneva Swift said after sweeping into my donut shop as though she owned the place. Momma had hired her a few weeks earlier to be her second in command for her diverse holdings after I'd turned the job down, and Geneva and I had been unhappy with each other from first sight. Maybe it was because she was younger, thinner, and, if I was being truthful about it, quite a bit prettier than I was. Then again, it could have been because she presented a façade to the outside world of overall competence, something I had never been able to do in my life. I was pretty good at a lot of things, but no one had ever accused me of being excellent at anything, with the single exception of donut making.

Then again, maybe we didn't get along because she was a jerk.

I tried to pull the papers out of Geneva's hand so I could read them first, but she held onto them with a grip stronger than I would have suspected her of having.

"Just sign them," she said with real aggravation in her voice. "You don't need to concern yourself with the content."

Boy, did she not know who she was dealing with. Ordering me around was the one sure way of getting me to dig my heels in. Geneva would have been much better off taking just about any other approach.

"I beg to differ," I said as I finally wrestled them away from her. A few of my customers had been looking on, but a quick glance in their direction from me was all that it took for them to find new fascination with the donuts and coffees in front of them. "*Franchise agreement*? What is this about, Geneva?"

Momma's assistant had told me the first time we'd met that she preferred to be referred to as Ms. Swift, and nothing else. Again, there had been something in her voice that had tasted more like an order than a request, so naturally, I had used her first name when speaking to her from the very beginning, no matter how many times she reminded me of her preference.

"It's something your mother has been considering, and I'm just covering all of the preliminary groundwork for her," Geneva said, making direct eye contact and defying me to argue with her.

I was more than happy to play that game. I pulled out my phone before she could object, and I dialed my mother's phone number.

It went straight to voice mail.

Geneva said smugly, "Oh, did I forget to mention that she's in meetings all day in Charlotte? So sorry for the confusion."

"Okay," I said as I dialed a second number, which clearly surprised my mother's new assistant.

The man in question answered on the third ring. "Hey, Suzanne. What's up?"

"Phillip," I said to my stepfather, "Geneva's here about a franchise agreement for Donut Hearts. She claims that it's Momma's idea. Do you know anything about it?"

"As a matter of fact, I'm the one who brought it up," he said a bit hesitantly.

"*What?*"

"Hang on a second, Suzanne. Let me explain. Your mother and I were talking the other day about how to generate some passive income for you from Donut Hearts, and I mentioned offhand that you could always franchise your name and some of your signature donuts. Your treats are way too tasty to keep from the rest of the world."

"Are you telling me that on your urging, she had franchising contracts drawn up without even *asking* me about it first?" I asked, trying to keep my voice as calm as I could. I could see Geneva's face whiten a bit and her lips tighten, so I had a feeling I was onto something.

"That's not the way it happened at all!" Phillip protested. "Dot said that she was going to talk to you about the idea when the time was right."

"Well, it's surely not now," I said. "If Momma wanted to discuss it with me first, then why did she send Geneva over here with something for me to sign?"

"I'm telling you that she didn't," Phillip said. "Call your mother right now so you can get this straightened out before it blows up into something too big to pull back in. No, that's right, she's in meetings in Charlotte all day. Hang on." Ten seconds later, he got back on the phone. "I texted her and told her to drop whatever she was doing and call you."

"She doesn't have to do that..." I said as my phone notified me that I had another phone call. "That's her. Gotta go."

"Let me know what happens," he said as I switched calls to Momma.

"What is so urgent, Suzanne?"

"It can wait, Momma," I apologized. "Geneva just came into Donut Hearts waving a stack of franchise papers in my face and demanding that I sign them. The truth is that it kind of caught me off guard."

"She did *what*?" Wow, there was a great deal of ice in those three words.

I had just started to explain again when the call abruptly ended. A moment later Geneva's phone rang, and the moment she realized it was my mother, her face lost the last vestiges of color it had sported earlier. "Yes, ma'am. No, ma'am. I was taking initiative. Yes, ma'am. I understand. I apologize." Geneva hung up the phone and shot me a venomous look for an instant before it morphed into a plastered-on fake smile. "My apologies, Suzanne. I misunderstood my directives."

I just bet she had. "No worries. I just wanted to clear things up," I answered.

"If you don't mind, I'll just take those and be on my way," she replied as she reached for the documents.

I was too quick for her, though. I pulled them away and tucked them behind the counter, where she couldn't get at them without coming through me. "Tell you what. I'll just hang on to those for a bit, if you don't mind."

Geneva clearly minded a lot, but after the scolding my mother must have just given her, she was obviously in no mood to test Momma's patience again so soon.

"As you wish," she said as she headed for the door.

"Care for a treat while you're here?" I asked her sweetly, albeit not sincerely. Geneva had turned down every offer of donuts I'd made to her since the first moment we'd met. Maybe *that* was why I didn't like her. There was just something I didn't trust about a person who would turn down a free donut. It might not have been fair, but hey, we all have our idiosyncrasies, and I was perfectly willing to live with mine.

Ten minutes later, Momma called me again.

Before she could say a word, I said, "Listen, everything's fine on this end. Honest. I know you're busy right now. You took care of it. We're good."

Momma whispered, "That's good to hear. The main reason I'm calling, though, is that I'm making this Neanderthal I'm dealing with stew a bit since he kept me waiting when I first got here. I wanted to call back to apologize for Geneva's behavior while I had a minute. She has a tendency to try to anticipate my needs and wants, and it's caused a few issues with us since she's come on board."

"Are you going to fire her?" I asked.

"Of course not. You don't get rid of a puppy when you're paper training them," Momma said, scolding me now instead of her assistant. Frankly, I liked it the other way around better. "She'll come around in time."

"Wow, I can't believe how patient you are with her," I told her.

"Suzanne, contrary to what you might believe, deep down, I'm quite a reasonable person."

"Hey, hang on one second. I never said that you were unreasonable."

"*Never?*" she asked archly.

Okay, she had me. Like I said earlier, I never claimed to be perfect. "You know what I mean," I said.

"I do. I'm just having a bit of fun with you," Momma said.

"Fun for who, exactly?"

"Why me, of course," she said with a soft laugh. "That should do it. I believe I've left him idle long enough. I wish I could send you a photo. He's the nicest shade of red. The man doesn't realize it yet, but his behavior has just cost him five thousand dollars. I'm raising my price on a property he must have simply because he's an oaf and needs a lesson in manners. Good bye, Suzanne."

"Bye," I said, but my phone was already dead. My mother had been known to charge more than that in the past as a jerk tax. It didn't pay to cross her, and everybody she did business with learned that lesson sooner or later. How expensive the class got depended on how long it took the other person to realize that there was more going on behind her petite exterior than met the eye.

I tried to wipe the entire mess out of my mind as I worked the last hour of the morning at Donut Hearts. It was finally starting to feel like home to me again, though I'd recently caught myself a few times wondering if it ever would. There were enough lulls to make me consider the idea of franchising my shop's distinctive name and recipes. Would there *really* be a market for that in other parts of the South? How about the country? The world? I had to slow myself down. I had many flaws, but possessing a delusion of grandeur wasn't one of them. The truth was that one shop was all that I cared about, and I planned to keep it that way. Still, it might not hurt to discuss the possibility with my husband, Jake.

The only problem was that he was out of town at the moment, working as a consultant for a small police department on the western edge of North Carolina. He was four hours away from April Springs, and besides, I knew that he had his hands full. The local sheriff's wife had died under suspicious circumstances, and the town council had hired Jake to step in and investigate. Evidently, there was quite a bit of intrigue going on, but I hadn't gotten much out of Jake so far. He worked his cases that way sometimes, not commenting to anyone about anything until he had a way into his investigation, not even me. In the meantime, I was working at Donut Hearts, doing the one thing that I did best in the world.

"The kitchen is clean. Can I take off now?" Emma asked me five minutes after we locked our doors for the day.

"Do you have an early class I don't know about?" I asked her.

Emma was taking some classes at the local community college while she worked for me. I'd encouraged it, since I would do anything to keep her at the donut shop. Not only was she a great assistant, but she was also a dear friend, and I dreaded the day she left me for good.

"No, Barton needs some help picking out some flatware for the restaurant, and since Mom and I are backing him, we're adding our input to everything but the menu."

Emma and her mother, Sharon, had inherited some money recently, and they'd tried to buy Donut Hearts. When I'd turned their generous offer down, they'd decided to put it into Emma's boyfriend's restaurant, which was sure money as far as I was concerned. I knew that a great many new business ventures failed in the first year—and that restaurants were even worse—but Barton was the most gifted chef I'd ever met, so if anyone could make it on the merits of his food, it was that man.

"Sure, you can take off."

"You really don't mind?" Emma asked me, clearly sensing that something was on my mind. "If you want to talk, I'm always here for you."

"Honestly, I'm fine. Now go before I change my mind," I said and grinned as I swatted at her with a hand towel. "Grace is at a sales conference in Sarasota, Jake is out of town on a case, and Momma is in Charlotte on business, so I've got nowhere else I need to be, and no one to be with." It sounded a bit pathetic when I said it out loud, so I quickly followed it up with, "The truth is that I'm looking forward to a nap and then maybe a walk around town later. Good luck."

"I'll need it," she said with a sigh. "It's hard to believe that three people could have such diverse and adamant opinions about what seems to be the most trivial stuff."

"Is starting a restaurant harder than you thought it would be?" I asked as I let her out through the front door.

"Yeah, but that doesn't mean that it's not fun," she said with the hint of a grin. "I'll see you tomorrow, Suzanne."

"Not if I see you first," I said with a smile of my own.

Once she was gone, I put on some Van Morrison and sang a bit as I finished my closing chores for the day. The singer never failed to lighten my mood, and by the time I locked up the shop for the day, I was ready and willing to go back to the cottage, grab a quick shower, and then take that nap I'd been promising myself all day.

Unfortunately, the world had other plans for me.

As I stepped outside of the shop and locked the door behind me, I heard a voice say, "Leaving so soon? I'd *love* to have your hours, Suzanne. It must be so freeing having your afternoons available to do whatever you wish to do."

I didn't even have to turn around to know who was talking to me.

Evidently Gabby Williams and I were going to have ourselves a little chat, whether it was on my schedule for the day or not.

Chapter 2

"GABBY, HOW NICE TO see you," I said. I wasn't even lying. Confounding folks everywhere, it was true that the stern woman had become a close friend of mine over the years, notwithstanding her general mood and demeanor, which could best be described as severe. "How's the building coming?" I asked as I glanced next door at the space where her shop, ReNEWed, was rising from the ashes of its former self, and I meant that literally.

"I should be able to have the grand reopening in the next six to seven weeks," she said. "That is, if I can get my new contractor to actually try to meet the deadlines I've given him."

It was difficult enough being friends with Gabby. I couldn't imagine trying to work for her. The contractor, a woman from Union Square, had my sympathies.

"I've never heard of a construction project coming in on time in my life unless my mother's count," I told her.

"I got Cynthia's name from Dot, as a matter of fact," Gabby said. "She came highly recommended, and I must say, I'm a bit disappointed so far."

That didn't sound like anyone Momma would endorse. I had a sudden thought. "Have you by any chance changed your mind about the shop's layout since she got started on finishing the build?" I asked her.

Gabby frowned. "Maybe, but they aren't *big* changes I'm asking for. Really, they should be quite simple to do. I don't know why she's been making such a fuss. What do I know about load-bearing walls and properly sized footings? That's *her* job, isn't it?"

It was all becoming clear, but I knew better than to try to argue the point with Gabby Williams. I was brave, but I was most certainly not stupid.

"I'm sure it will all work out in the end," I told her with more confidence than I really felt. "Was there something I could do for you?"

"As a matter of fact, there is," Gabby said. "How difficult would it be for you to whip up three dozen pumpkin donut holes for me?"

"It's not pumpkin donut season at Donut Hearts," I told her. I kept a few items seasonal so folks would have a reason to come by, but I was beginning to question that policy. Pumpkin donuts were turning out to be some of the most popular items on my menu.

"I understand that, but I'm sure you can make an exception for me," Gabby said confidently.

"When would you need them?" I asked her.

"Why, now, of course. You're closed for the day, and I know Jake is out of town, as well as Grace and your mother. I can't imagine you have anything else to do. Actually, I'm doing you a favor by giving you a task to complete."

I looked at her and laughed, but then I realized that she was dead serious. "Gabby, I've been here since four a.m. I've already worked my shift at Donut Hearts for the day."

She frowned. "Of course. I'm sorry. I should have realized. I hate to lie to someone I care about, but I'll just tell him that I couldn't make it happen."

She turned to go, and I thought about letting her walk away, but I just couldn't bring myself to do it. "Hang on. Fine. I give in."

Gabby turned. "No, it's perfectly all right. I overstepped. I understand."

"I already said that I'd do it," I told her. "Do you feel like keeping me company while I make them?"

Gabby had the nerve to look at her watch. "I'm not sure. I don't have a great deal of time. Will it take long?"

I was a hair's breath away from telling her that I had changed my mind yet again, but I knew that would get me more grief than just refusing her outright in the first place would have accomplished. "Not long. I can have you out the door in an hour."

"That long?" she asked critically. "Are they really that complicated to make?"

"Not necessarily, but I also have to heat the oil back up."

"Can't you just bake them or something?" she asked me.

"That used oven I put in for baked donuts is on the fritz again," I answered.

Emma and Sharon had persuaded me to buy it so we could try yet a third type of donut to go along with our cake and yeast donuts. We'd sold a few baked ones, but they hadn't caught on yet, whether they were a healthier alternative or not. Most folks didn't come to Donut Hearts to take care of themselves, but I'd been willing to try it to keep the ladies happy.

"You really should buy a new one," Gabby said as I unlocked the front door.

"Cool. I'll pick one out of the catalogue and send you the bill," I said brightly.

"You wouldn't dare," Gabby answered severely.

"Of course I wouldn't. I was just teasing you," I said as I flipped on the fryer. At least the oil wasn't entirely cold yet. Maybe I could even shave a few minutes off my earlier estimate.

As I mixed the batter for the pumpkin donuts, Gabby took the only comfortable seat in the kitchen and watched me work. At least I wouldn't have to use the new donut dropper. I'd ruined the old one, and I still had trouble getting used to its replacement. "Don't you have to roll those out or something?" she asked.

"No, I've got a special gizmo made just for donut holes. A friend of mine found it and sent it to me. It's kind of cool, really."

"Do you use it for all of your donuts?" she asked, interested despite her aloof nature.

"The holes from the yeast donuts come naturally," I said as I grabbed a rolling form and showed it to her. "These cut out the donut rounds, and the dough left behind becomes the holes. Since I don't roll out the battered donuts, I have to create holes another way."

"That seems as though it's a great deal of trouble," Gabby said critically.

"It's really not, though. My customers like them, and I try to give them what they want."

After the pumpkin batter was finished, I decided to fry up some donuts too, as a special treat just for me. After all, nobody was around to count my calories, and I truly was addicted to the things.

"Bully for you," Gabby said. "I myself have another business model."

"What might that be?" I was almost afraid to ask.

"I make them feel fortunate to even be shopping in my store. That way they're grateful for *whatever* I allow them to purchase."

I thought she was joking again, but there was no smile on her face as she said it.

"Okay, that *is* different from mine." I checked the oil and saw that it was nearly at the proper temperature. "Do you mind if I ask you who these are for?" I really wasn't expecting her to answer, but I figured it would be fun making her squirm a bit.

"Suzanne, can you keep a secret?" she asked me furtively.

"You know I can," I answered. Was she really going to tell me?

"So can I," Gabby said with a grin. "You may ask, but I reserve the right whether to answer or not."

"Understood," I said with a smile of my own.

I figured it was real progress to get Gabby to even tease with me. She was certainly in a good mood, and I had to wonder if these holes might be for a new gentleman caller of hers. She hadn't had the greatest of luck in the romance department, but at least some of that could have had something to do with her crusty nature and generally snotty demeanor. I'd heard that some men enjoyed that kind of treatment, but they wouldn't have been any I'd care to know.

After the donut holes were finished, I put them through the glaze and then started on some rounds while the oil was still hot.

"I said holes, not donuts," Gabby told me, scolding me a bit.

"These aren't for you," I told her, matching her tone exactly.

"My mistake," Gabby answered.

I glanced over to see if she was angry with me, but instead, she looked pleased with my response. Maybe that was the best way to get on her good side, by consciously appealing to her gruff nature, returning like with like.

"Are those ready?"

"Let's give them a few minutes to cool so they don't stick together in the bag," I said as I finished up the batter by making four rounds. They would make a perfect snack for me later, and I was suddenly glad that Gabby had come in with her unreasonable demand.

After the four rounds were out of the hot oil, I glazed them as well and then quickly washed the dishes I'd just dirtied.

"Don't you have a dishwasher?" Gabby asked me, a bit appalled by my hand labor.

"I don't have the money to buy one, and if I did, I wouldn't have any place to put it," I said. "Besides, cleanup is easy enough."

"I don't know how you continue to function in these primitive conditions, Suzanne."

"With a bright smile and a song in my heart, I hope," I answered.

Gabby decided not to comment on that at all.

Once everything was spotless and the fryer was turned off again, I bagged the holes she'd requested. Before I handed them to her, I asked, "Would you like to know my fee?"

"I'm prepared to pay for your services," she said stiffly.

"Good. The only cost to you today is not to tell anyone I did this for you. I don't want to make it a habit of whipping up a batch of donuts every time a friend of mine gets an itch for treats."

"I understand that, but I need to pay you something," Gabby insisted.

"Nope, I won't take it. But this was a one-time deal. The *next* time you request a special order, it's going to cost you triple my usual fee."

"What about your friend-and-family rate?" Gabby asked me with a smile she tried her best to hide.

"That *is* the special rate. Everybody else has to pay *five* times the usual amount."

"Then this is a bargain indeed," she said as she took the offered treats.

I bagged up the four solo pumpkin donuts and walked her out.

"Are you still open?" Paige Hill asked me as she walked past the shop. After glancing at her phone for the time, she added, "Hey, I thought you closed an hour ago."

"I had to come back for something," I said with a grin that Gabby couldn't see.

"Well, I must be going," Gabby said. "Thank you, Suzanne. Good day, Paige."

"Good day to you, Gabby," Paige said, suppressing a grin.

My harsh friend studied her for a moment, nodded briskly, and then she walked away.

"What was that all about?" Paige asked me once Gabby was out of earshot.

"I could tell you, but then I'd have to kill you," I answered with a grin.

"Then don't tell me. Please. I mean it," Paige answered with the smile that she'd been hiding earlier. "Is that all that's left from today?"

"Why, are you hungry?" I asked her as she eyed the bag in my hand covetously.

"I skipped breakfast," Paige admitted.

"Here. You can have them," I said, feeling a momentary pang for what I was giving up but then realizing that I could always make more. Not today, but tomorrow, anyway.

Paige opened the bag and breathed deeply. "Pumpkin? I thought they were out of season."

"They are, so keep your voice down," I told her. "I had to make some as a special order, so I ran a few extras off for me, but you're welcome to them."

"I couldn't do that to you," Paige said, still looking at the bag.

"Tell you what. I don't need four, anyway. If you've got coffee at the bookstore, I'll split these with you," I told her. Suddenly, I didn't feel like being alone, and if I had anyone to choose out of all of the folks left in town, Paige would be high on my list, and that was saying something.

"It's a deal," she answered as she dove in and retrieved one. "Ooh, they're still warm."

"They are," I told her as we walked across Springs Drive and up the steps to her bookstore, The Last Page. We'd both named our businesses after ourselves, something I really liked about small-town living.

"Oh my gosh. Suzanne, this is amazing," she said as she took another bite.

"Tell you what. Just save one for me, and the rest are all yours," I said with a smile.

"Sorry," Paige said with a grin. "You know what? That's a big fat lie. I'm not sorry at all. You've got yourself a deal."

We walked up the steps to the front door, and Rita Delacourte greeted us. "Ladies," she said with a smile.

"Would you like a donut, Rita?" I offered her. After all, one wasn't that much to miss. "I brought one just for you."

"Thank you, but I'm meeting a friend for lunch," she said as she grabbed her purse. "Is it okay if I go now, Boss?"

"It's more than okay," Paige said. "Thanks for watching the place while I took a walk. Did I miss anything while I was gone?"

Rita paused, glanced at me, and then said, "No."

Paige and I both caught it. Rita was not cut out for lying, which made her okay in my book.

"Rita," Paige insisted.

"Well, *something* happened. I'm just not sure what it was."

"I'm listening," Paige said.

"Let's talk about it after lunch, if it's all that same to you. I'm going to be late as it is."

Paige nodded. "Okay, but we're having this conversation the minute you get back. Do you understand?"

"Yes, Boss," she said, clearly relieved to be getting out of there without disclosing what had happened earlier that had bothered her.

"What was that all about?" I asked once she was gone.

"I have no earthly idea," Paige replied.

"There was a mention of coffee earlier?" I asked her.

"Coming right up," she answered.

After Paige poured us both cups, we found a window seat in the sunshine. It was cold enough outside to make it a coveted spot, but since the bookstore wasn't crowded, we were able to snag it.

"How's business?" I asked her as I glanced around the shop.

"It's absolutely booming. Can't you tell?" Paige answered with a grin.

"I'm so sorry," I replied. "I know how it can be. I hit slumps all of the time."

"Don't worry about this," Paige answered. "I'm really doing fine. We have an online presence now that's making up for it when foot traffic is slow, so I'm not worried."

"Maybe I should try selling my donuts online," I joked.

"You can always try, but even places like Voodoo Donuts gave up on that dynamic," she said. "I'll do whatever I can to help you make it work, though, if you want to try my business model."

"I was halfway kidding," I told her. "How do you know about Voodoo Donuts? I'm in the business, so I've been aware of them for ages, but you run a bookstore."

"I went to Universal Studios in Orlando with my niece last year, and there was one on the walk from the park to the hotel every day. Naturally, we stopped in, and by the time we left, we were both addicted. I've even got a magnet on my fridge at home."

"I've always wanted to try that place," I told her. "I want to visit the mother ship in Oregon, though."

"You should get Jake to take you," she said. "I bet you could even write the trip off as a business expense," Paige said with a smile.

"Imagine that," I told her. "Maybe when things slow down. If they ever do. You'll never believe what happened to me today."

"You sold out of your donut run?" she asked as she took a bite of pumpkin donut. "I have no problem believing that at all."

"Momma's assistant came by the shop with franchising paperwork for me to sign," I told her.

"You're going to *franchise*?" she asked with almost a shriek.

"No. That's the point. Phillip suggested it offhand to Momma, and her snoopy new assistant decided to run with the idea without anyone's approval. I had to put a stop to it to let her know not to try to bully me into anything that wasn't my idea in the first place."

"What did you do, pour ice water over her head, or ram her car with your Jeep?" Paige asked with a laugh.

"Neither. I called my mother," I said.

It sounded a bit petulant when I said it, and I wondered if I might not have overreacted a bit based on the way I felt about the woman. I didn't have any *real* reason not to like Geneva, even though she was working closely with my mother. Maybe I *was* a little jealous. Then again, I'd been offered that spot and I'd turned it down, so what did I have to be jealous about?

"Suzanne, you didn't," Paige said, the smile suddenly vanishing. "That's kind of harsh, isn't it?"

"Probably," I said. "I'm starting to think I might owe her an apology."

"You *think*?" Paige asked. "I can't imagine how your mother must have reacted."

"I didn't hear what was said, but I was there when Geneva took the call. Her face went as white as a sheet. Blast it all, I'm going to have to grovel and ask her for her forgiveness, aren't I?"

Paige slapped my shoulder lightly. "Look at you, being a grown-up and everything. I'm so proud of you."

She was clearly being sarcastic, but I didn't act as though I knew it. "Thank you. I am something special, aren't I?" When I saw her looking at me oddly, I quickly added, "I'm kidding. I'll handle it later."

"Later?" Paige asked me with her eyebrows both raised.

"Later," I echoed firmly. "I'm going to need a hot shower, a nap, and maybe something else to eat before I tackle that particular item on my to-do list." I finished my coffee and stood. "Thanks for the chat."

"You don't have to leave. I didn't mean to run you off," the bookstore owner said.

"You didn't. I just realized how tired I was. I'll see you later."

As I started for the door, she stood and followed me. "Suzanne, we should have dinner sometime, just the two of us."

"That sounds lovely," I told her. "Were you thinking in the abstract, or are you free tonight?"

Paige looked at me and started laughing. "Tonight sounds great. Where should we go? Don't tell Trish I said this, but sometimes I get tired of the Boxcar day in and day out."

"Your secret is safe with me. The only problem is that I can't go far at night since my curfew is so early," I explained. "It's one of the perils of making donuts for a living."

"I can get Rita to cover the night shift, so we can go as early as four if you'd like," Paige answered.

"Four? I'm not *that* old," I said.

"Sorry, I didn't mean to offend you."

"You didn't," I replied with a grin. "I normally don't eat until four thirty."

Paige looked at me quizzically. "I'm not sure how to react to that."

"I get that a lot," I told her. "We should go to Napoli's," I decided suddenly. I hadn't seen Angelica or the girls in quite a while, so it would be good to catch up with them again.

"That sounds amazing," Paige answered. "Should I pick you up at the cottage?"

"Why don't I drive?" I countered. "I'll bring the Jeep around at four."

"I didn't think you ate that early," she reminded me.

"Hey, in my defense, it takes half an hour to get there," I told her.

"Okay, four it is," Paige said. "Is it wrong that I'm already excited about eating there this evening?"

"I think the only thing wrong would be if you weren't," I told her. "See you then."

"Bye," she said as three customers walked into the shop past us. "See?" she asked with a grin. "I'm fine."

"I never doubted that for a second," I answered happily.

I glanced at my watch and saw that I had plenty of time to do everything I wanted to do on my list before it was time to pick Paige up for our girls'-night dinner out. The shower was definitely first on my list, though. The smell of donuts, no matter how enticing some folks found it, permeated everything from my clothes to my skin to my hair, and I couldn't wait to get clean again. After that, I'd get a small bite for lunch, maybe just cheese and crackers to tide me over until later, and finally a nap. If I still had the inclination, the energy, and the conscience, I'd try to find Geneva to apologize for my behavior earlier.

I might not try that hard, but I'd at least try.

Somehow, the afternoon flew by, and it was time to pick Paige up at the bookstore. I hadn't gotten around to apologizing to Geneva, and I honestly did feel a little bad about it, but not bad enough to postpone our dinner out together. As I grabbed my keys, my cell phone rang.

I nearly jumped for joy when I saw that it was my husband. "Jake! You *never* call this early. What's up?"

"I had a free minute, so I wanted to touch base with you," he said. "I'm a little unhappy about leaving you there all alone."

"As much as I appreciate your concern, I happen to have dinner plans for tonight, so there's no need to worry about me," I told him.

After a momentary pause, he said, "Have fun, but remind the guy that I carry a gun, would you? I would hate for him to get any ideas."

I had to laugh at that. "Paige and I are going to Napoli's for dinner, just us girls," I replied.

"Wow, now I really *am* jealous," Jake answered, and it was true enough that I could hear it in his voice.

"Would you be more jealous if I was eating dinner with a guy at the Boxcar Grill or going to Napoli's with Paige?" I asked him. When he didn't answer, I asked, "Jake? Are you still there?"

"Give me a second. I'm thinking," he answered.

I loved that my once-always-so-serious husband was finally starting to really enjoy teasing me about things like that. He'd had some pretty harsh blows in life, and when we'd first met, he hadn't been all that playful, but since then, I'd become a good—or some might say bad—influence on him. He'd definitely loosened up, at least a little bit.

"Liar," I said. "You knew the answer as soon as I asked it."

"What can I say? I'd be more jealous of the guy, but not because I was worried about you. I would just wish that it was me across the table from you, not somebody else."

"Hey, you are doing important work," I reminded him. "Do I even need to ask how the investigation is going?"

He replied, "It snowed a little last night, but today has been pretty nice. That's not to say that we won't get more flurries tonight."

I laughed. "I get it. You don't want, or you can't, talk about it. Message received, loud and clear." I was already in front of the bookstore, darn that short commute, so I added, "I'm at The Last Page, so I'd better go. Take care, my love."

"Right back at you, times two," he answered.

"How can I possibly get into trouble eating at Napoli's with a friend?" I asked him.

"I don't know, but if anybody can do it, it's my lovely wife."

He hung up before I had a chance to retort, which was just as well.

After all, it was hard to argue with the man when he was right.

Chapter 3

"YOU'RE RIGHT ON TIME," Paige said as she got into my Jeep.

"Hey, no offense, but if you weren't standing on the porch like you were when I pulled up, I would have already left without you. Napoli's waits for no man, or woman, either," I answered.

"I wouldn't be able to fault you for that," she said with a laugh.

As we drove to Union Square, I asked her, "So, why was Rita so mysterious before?"

"Apparently, someone came by the shop looking for me," Paige said with a frown.

"You're the owner. Is that really all that odd?" I asked as I passed city hall. Our mayor, and my good friend, George Morris, was standing outside talking to a man I didn't know. When he saw me, he smiled and waved, which I returned with gusto.

"Who was that with the mayor?" Paige asked me.

"I have no idea," I answered.

She looked at me oddly. "Seriously? I thought you knew everybody in April Springs."

"Not everybody, and not their brother, either," I replied.

"Sorry. My mistake," Paige said quickly. "I didn't mean to hit a nerve there."

"You didn't. Well, actually, you did, but it's not important. Most folks think I'm connected in April Springs with every last resident, but unless they like donuts, there's a chance I don't know them."

Paige looked at me with mock surprise on her face. "Hang on one second. Are you telling me that there are people in our town who *don't* like donuts? I'm having trouble believing that, Suzanne."

"It's true nonetheless," I told her, grinning at her histrionics.

"I'll have to take your word for it, but if there actually *is* such a person, I don't care to know them," Paige said.

"Then don't meet Geneva Swift," I told her.

Paige shrugged. "I've already had the pleasure, if you can call it that. Anyway, at least that explains that. I've got a hunch now why you don't like her."

"It can't be as obvious as that, can it?" I asked her.

"Hey, I don't have much patience with folks who brag about *not* reading," she answered. "To me, it's as necessary as breathing and sleeping."

"Me too," I echoed. "Anyway, back to Rita. Tell me more about this mysterious stranger who came looking for you."

"That's just it," she said. "Rita said that he was the embodiment of Mr. Darcy from *Pride and Prejudice*—dark, brooding, and handsome—but I'm at a loss as to who it might be."

"Well, based on that description alone, I'd like to meet him myself. Did she have any other clues for you as to the man's identity?"

"No. He just told her that he'd come back later, and then he walked out. She said he didn't even glance at a book on the way in or out. Evidently, he was intent on seeing me or nothing at all."

"I can see that," I told her.

"Well, I can't. Can you imagine the circumstances you would *ever* walk into a bookstore without at least glancing at stray title or two, let alone pick up something and leaf through it?"

"I can't," I told her honestly. "So, you're not at least a *little* bit intrigued by that description?"

"Maybe a little," she admitted. "It's been a while since I've had a date with anyone I was really interested in. April Springs isn't exactly a hotbed of eligible men our age."

"I can imagine," I answered.

"You would have to, wouldn't you? I don't blame you. If I had Jake, I couldn't fathom the circumstances that would make me look at another man." She blushed a bit as she said it. "I didn't mean for that to sound the way it must have sounded to you."

"Hey, I think he's the best too," I said. "Would you like my help trying to find *you* someone?"

"Thanks but no thanks. I'd rather do it on my own, if it's all the same to you."

"No worries, my friend," I told her.

We were nearing Napoli's and I couldn't wait to see everyone again. Eating would be a nice bonus too, but the company was what really mattered.

At least that was what I kept telling myself as I did everything but wipe the drool off my face as we drove into the full parking lot.

Then I spotted someone getting into a truck in the parking lot that I did not want to see.

"Duck down," I told Paige as I pulled into a spot and did the same.

She did as I asked. "Suzanne, is there someone who shouldn't see us out having dinner together? I thought this was all perfectly innocent."

"It is. I just saw Geneva Swift, and the last thing I need right now is another run-in with that woman," I explained.

As I tried to look above the dash, I struggled to make out who she was with, but from where I'd had to park so quickly, I couldn't tell. She'd gotten into a pickup truck passenger door, which didn't eliminate many folks at all in April Springs, men and women alike. Trucks seemed to be the vehicles of choice for a great many folks in our area, whether they were used for hauling plywood, manure, or groceries.

"I take it you haven't apologized to her yet," Paige said.

"I didn't have time," I said as I watched the truck drive away.

I couldn't make out the model from as far away as we were, and I wouldn't even be able to swear to the exact color, given my quick glance. It might have been green, blue, or even possibly gray.

"You could have done it in the parking lot just then," Paige said as she saw me sitting up in my seat again.

"Coulda, woulda, shoulda," I said, sounding more like a kid than I'd meant to. "I can always do it tomorrow," I added as I opened my door.

"Now, are you just going to sit there all night, or are we going to go eat dinner?" I asked with a grin.

"I choose dinner, each and every time," she said.

"Suzanne, Paige, how lovely to see you both," Antonia DeAngelis said the moment we walked in. She pulled me aside. "Can you talk to my mother? She's acting like a crazy woman for some reason, and none of us know what to do with her."

Angelica DeAngelis was a true force of nature, and if her daughters couldn't deal with her, I wasn't sure there was anything I could do, but that didn't mean that I wouldn't try. "What's going on?"

"That's the problem. She won't tell us," Antonia said. "You have a way with her that we never have. As a matter of fact, I was talking with Maria the other day about how you were an honorary DeAngelis sister."

"Laying it on a little thick, aren't you?" I asked her with a grin.

"Too much?" she asked, smiling back at me and clearly not one bit affronted by my chiding her.

"Just a bit," I replied as I held up my index finger and thumb about three inches apart. "Who's back there with her now?"

"Sophia," she said, "but I'm not sure how much more she can take."

Sophia was the baby of the crew and also the most like her mother, at least in general temperament. She also came the closest to matching Angelica's skills in the kitchen, something the other girls grudgingly admitted.

"I'll see what I can do," I said as I turned to Paige. "I'll be right there. I'm sure Antonia won't mind finding us a table."

"I'm on it," she said with a grin. "Just don't make me go into that kitchen with you."

"Should I come with you?" Paige offered despite the look of trepidation on her face as she said it.

"I appreciate the offer, but I need to do this on my own," I told her, and then, before I could chicken out, I walked into the kitchen.

Without looking up, Angelica said, "You'd better have a good excuse coming back here."

"I didn't realize that I needed one," I told her, and then I nodded to Sophia, who shook her head abruptly, trying to warn me off.

I decided to ignore it.

"Oh, it's you. Hello, Suzanne."

Angelica didn't say it with much warmth, and I decided if I was going to do her any good at all, I needed to shock her a bit, as dangerous a tactic as that might be. The last thing I wanted was to be banned from Napoli's, and I wasn't sure that Jake would ever forgive me, even if I could someday learn to forgive myself.

"Since when have you been so rude to your guests, let alone your friends?" I asked her, putting a whip in my voice as I spoke.

Sophia's face went white as she raced for the pantry to get out of the direct line of fire.

"What did you just say?" Angelica looked at me, the fire clear in her eyes.

"You heard me. Clearly *somebody* put a burr under your saddle. Do you want to talk about it with an old friend, or do I need to find someplace else to eat tonight?" I held her stare, but it was all that I could do not to flinch.

Angelica started to say something, and then she thought better of it. After a few seconds, she nodded and called out, "Sophia, Suzanne and I will be out back for a minute. The kitchen is yours." Then she turned to me and shook a finger in my face. "You, come with me."

Apparently I'd chosen the wrong approach, and I was about to pay for it. I hated when the truism bit me on the rump that no good deed went unpunished, and I had a feeling that I was about to get another reminder of its universal wisdom.

I followed her outside, and as I glanced back at Sophia, there was a look of pure fright on her face.

It was exactly the way I felt on the inside, but I knew that I couldn't show any weakness, or I'd be lost.

The moment the heavy steel door behind us hissed shut, I braced myself for a barrage.

Instead, Angelica embraced me and started crying.

I would have rather been scolded.

"What happened? What's wrong?" I asked her as I stroked her back gently. "It's going to be okay, Angelica. Is it one of the girls? Is someone in trouble? I can help, no matter how bad it might be."

"What if I need help burying a body?" she asked me as she pulled away and wiped at her tears.

"Well, I'm going to assume that whoever did it deserved it. I'd rather call Jake and get his spin on things, but if you think the only way out of this is to get rid of the evidence, let me pull my Jeep around. We'll need to borrow a shovel, but I think I know where I can find one."

Angelica looked at me seriously. "You would do that for me?"

"If the circumstances dictate it, I'm *always* going to give you the benefit of the doubt."

She met my earnest expression with one of her own. "You knew I was speaking metaphorically, didn't you?"

"I was kind of hoping that was the case," I admitted, "but the offer still stands. Now, who are we going to bury, and why do they deserve it?"

"Your friend, the mayor, stood me up tonight," Angelica said.

"Okay, maybe you should take a deep breath and tell me more than that. Did he have a reason?"

"He claimed that all of a sudden, he had a meeting with someone from out of town, but it sounded as though he was just trying to avoid seeing me," Angelica said. "I thought things were going well between us, and then he pulls a stunt like that."

I said earnestly, "When Paige and I left April Springs, George was talking to a stranger in front of city hall."

"Was this 'stranger' pretty?" she asked me.

"His mother might think so, but I didn't," I answered. "Angelica, what's gotten into you? You're an accomplished, talented, beautiful, successful woman, but you're acting like a silly teenager. It's not like you."

"That's quite the list of attributes you just gave me," Angelica said, "but I'm afraid I don't deserve it. You're right. I'm acting like a fool."

"How *are* things between you and George?" I asked, risking incurring another bout of anger, or worse yet, tears, from her.

"I thought we were doing amazingly well, but the last several days, he's been acting odd, as though he has troubles on his mind," Angelica answered. "I'm afraid I listened to my daughters as they recounted time after time the same thing had happened to them, and they'd ended up being dumped, or worse yet, cheated on, by one of the young men they'd been dating."

"Have you considered the possibility that George's behavior has nothing to do with you and that he really *does* have troubles on his mind?" I asked her.

"No, somehow that concept escaped me," she answered with a wry grin. "And when I should have been offering him my support, I've been acting like a petulant little brat. I'm afraid I owe him an apology."

"That I couldn't say, but I'd give George some slack. He's one of the good ones. You can trust him, you know." I felt in my heart that it was true. I had trusted George Morris with my life on more than one occasion, and I wouldn't hesitate to do so it again if the need arose.

"I know that. My husband betrayed me, and the closer I get to George, the more I fear it will happen again. Max cheated on you, and yet you trust Jake with your whole heart. How do you do that?"

"That's just it. I knew that I couldn't blame Jake for something that happened before we'd ever met, and I decided that even though I was taking a risk trusting a man again, it was one I was willing to take. Just for the record, he hasn't given me any reason to doubt him, and I know George wouldn't give you one, either."

She nodded. "Thank you for being my friend," Angelica said as she hugged me again, though this one was quite a bit dryer since she'd gotten over her crying spell.

"Thank you right back," I told her with a smile.

"Are you here alone? I heard Jake was out of town," Angelica said.

"He is. I brought Paige Hill with me," I said.

"She's a lovely girl, isn't she?" Angelica asked. "I'm glad the two of you are friends."

"So am I," I said. "Now, if we're finished out here, it's getting kind of chilly, and you don't even have a jacket on."

"My anger kept me warm," Angelica said with a smile as she led me back inside.

Three daughters were standing there, staring at the door, as we walked through. It was clear they were trying to decide whether they should brave their mother's wrath to try to save me or let me fend for myself.

I wouldn't have done anything any differently if I'd been in their shoes.

In a flash Sophia, suddenly got very interested in the large stockpot simmering on the stove, while Antonia and Maria nearly dove out the door of the kitchen into the dining room.

"Is everything okay?" Sophia was brave enough to ask.

"It's fine," Angelica said as she touched her daughter's shoulder lightly and smiled. "I'm sorry," she added softly.

I could see a sarcastic remark start to form in Sophia's mind, but she quickly, and wisely, bit it back. "No worries, Mom. We all have those kinds of days."

Angelica nodded and then turned to me. "Suzanne, if you'll excuse me for a second, I need a word with the girls out front."

"I'll be right here," I said, and Angelica disappeared.

The moment she was gone, Sophia put down the ladle in her hand and started bowing to me, waving her arms in the air in supplication.

"Stop that," I said with a laugh. "You look ridiculous."

"I'm completely sincere," she answered, though she did stop gesturing. "You confronted the beast and lived to tell about it. You are my hero. How did you do it?"

I wasn't about to share the conversation I'd just had with Angelica. "I won't tell you, but feel free to ask your mother."

"No way is *that* happening," Sophia said as she shook her head. "For what it's worth, thanks. I wouldn't have believed it if I hadn't seen it with my own two eyes."

"You're welcome," I told her as Angelica came back into the kitchen.

"What were you welcoming her for?" she asked me.

"She wanted a weather report, so I gave her an update," I said with a smile.

"Yes, I'm sure that was it," Angelica answered, clearly not buying it for a second. "I've already gotten Paige's approval, so all I need is yours. I'm going to be handling your dinner tonight personally, and if you have a problem with that or with me picking up the check, I'm afraid we're going to have to go back outside, Suzanne."

Angelica looked as though she meant it, and I'd already gambled and won once. There was no way I was going to push my luck again. "Whatever you say is fine with me," I answered her with a smile.

She smiled broadly. "Excellent," she answered, and then she turned to Sophia. "Why can't you girls be that agreeable with me?"

Before Sophia could get herself into trouble, I decided that it was time to flee while I still could. "I'll be at my table if you need me," I told them both.

They nodded at me in exactly the same way, with the same rhythm and motion, and it had never been more clear to me that they were indeed mother and daughter.

I got out of there.

After all, I'd already done what I could, and I was even hungrier now than I had been before.

Knowing Angelica, though, that wasn't going to be a problem soon.

Chapter 4

"I'M GLAD YOU'RE DRIVING," Paige told me as we started to make our way back to April Springs. "I am one stuffed turkey."

"I know exactly what you mean. I can't believe we didn't even have room for dessert," I told her. "Not that it was a problem. Angelica packed enough for us to eat for a week, including treats."

"What exactly did you do, Suzanne, save her life in the war or something?" Paige asked me as the darkness filled the air.

I loved this time of year. It gave me the perfect excuse to go to bed without apologizing to anyone. The height of summer was another story entirely. Then, the sun was blazing in all of its glory when I had to pull the blackout curtains in order to have any hope of resting at all.

"Nothing," I said simply.

"That meal was many things, but nothing wasn't one of them. I've been trying to pick a favorite from the entrée sampler she made for us, but I keep thinking of new reasons to come up with a different answer."

"It's almost a push, but the ravioli has always been my favorite," I told her, happy to skirt the issue of my private conversation with Angelica.

I was glad Paige decided to leave it alone. I decided to change the subject. "So, I wonder who your mysterious Mr. Darcy is."

"He's probably an overweight salesman from Charlotte trying to get me to buy a new rug for the shop," she answered with a laugh. "Rita has more of a vivid imagination than the authors whose books we stock in the shop."

"Is she really that bad?" I asked, keeping my eyes on the road.

"She's worse, if that's possible," Paige said. "A few weeks ago, she told me this intricate story about how a woman had saved her life by stopping her from walking into traffic."

"That could have happened," I said.

"On Springs Drive?" she countered. "We're not exactly known for our heavy traffic, and besides, I saw the entire thing through the window. George Morris was driving that truck of his under the speed limit, if you can believe that. Terri Milner tapped her on the shoulder to ask her a question about a book she had on order, and Rita took it as a sign from above that her life was charmed, somehow."

"Well, there are worse things than a good imagination to have in her job," I said.

"I know that, but I wish the woman would spend less time reading and more time dusting the shelves and waiting on customers," Paige said. "Not that I don't sneak a peek at a book now and then myself," she added a bit guiltily.

"That's different, though. You're the boss," I told her.

"It does all come down to that, doesn't it? We are in similar positions. I have just one full-time employee just like you do, but sometimes, it feels as though the weight of the world is on my shoulders."

"I get that," I told her. "I look at it this way. We provide valuable services to the good people of April Springs. You feed their souls, and I cater to their sweet teeth. Between the two of us, we've got it covered, and usually, they don't have to wait two or three days to get either one of our goods."

"Unless it's a special order," Paige reminded me.

"I know, but anyone looking for something to read can probably find it in your shop. They just might not realize that they wanted it before they came in," I told her.

"I suppose you're right," she answered as we came into the city limits of April Springs.

No matter how many times I left, and no matter how long I was gone, I was always happy to get back. That probably made me a rube in some folks' opinion, but I didn't care.

"Where should I drop you?" I asked her. "The bookstore or home?"

"I want to go home, take a hot bath, and then go to bed," she told me. As I started to turn up her street, she said, "But I have to go back to The Last Page."

"Okay dokey," I said as I truncated the turn and swung back onto Springs Drive. There wasn't a soul out on the road but us, so it wasn't as daring as it sounded.

We stopped on the road between our shops, and I turned on my emergency blinkers. "Let me get you some of those leftovers."

"I couldn't possibly take any, especially since Angelica wouldn't let us pay. Those are all yours, my friend."

I glanced back at all of the food we'd taken out with us. "Are you sure? I'm happy to share, and there's plenty for both of us."

"I'm sure. I couldn't live with the temptation, knowing that all of that great food was just a few footsteps away. I don't know how you do it."

"Mostly I don't," I answered her with a grin. "That's how I manage to keep my girlish figure, which is getting more girlish by the hour."

"I think you're perfect just the way you are," Paige said as she headed to her shop.

"You seriously don't want any of this?" I asked her again in the nippy night air.

"Want? Oh, yes. Need? No, ma'am. It's all yours."

"All right. I'm not going to keep trying to twist your arm," I told her. "If you change your mind later, it will probably be too late," I added with a grin.

"If you can polish off those bags, then more power to you," she laughed.

Rita was waiting at the door for her, but she couldn't even wait to come back in. "Thank goodness you're here," she said, nearly panting from excitement.

"What's going on? Did I miss something while I was gone?"

"No, but you were about to. Mr. Darcy is inside."

"Don't you dare go inside without me," I said as I pulled the Jeep in front of Donut Hearts. The food would be fine in the cool night air, and there was no way I was going to just leave with something so exciting going on right under my nose.

Paige waited, a little impatiently it looked like to me, and as soon as I joined her, a handsome and dark man with brooding eyes came outside.

"Richard," Paige said, "What on earth are you doing here?"

It wasn't the warmest welcome I'd ever witnessed in my life.

Apparently Paige and Richard had some kind of history together.

"Excuse me. I'm going to head home now," I said as I started back across the street.

"Suzanne, you don't need to go anywhere. Richard was just leaving," Paige said, and then she turned to the handsome man. "Isn't that right, Richard?"

"I'm not going anywhere until you talk to me," he insisted. "I miss you, and you need to hear my side of the story, Paige."

"Funny, but I don't think I do," she told him.

"You can't keep this grudge you've got going forever," he said angrily.

"Oh no? Just watch me. In the meantime, stay out of my bookstore. You're not welcome here," Paige added sharply as she started for her shop's front door. When she saw Rita lingering and looking absolutely torn about what to do next, she asked, "Are you coming, or should I sign you out for the night?"

"I'm right behind you, ma'am," Rita said as she made an apologetic shrug in Richard's direction.

"I can't believe that woman," he said, mostly to himself after they were both gone.

I didn't even know how to begin to address that, so I walked back to the Jeep, making my escape.

"Hey, you. Suzanne. Hang on a second. I want to talk to you," he told me.

I stopped and turned with car keys in my hand held between my fingers like the claws of a cat, ready to strike. "I don't have anything to say to you."

"You're just going to take her side without even hearing what I have to say?" Richard asked me.

"Absolutely. That's going to happen ten times out of ten, and you got it on the first guess."

"You women *always* stick together, don't you?" he asked angrily.

I hadn't known the man for more than two minutes, and I was already tired of him. Whatever he'd done to Paige, there was no doubt in my mind that he richly deserved it. "*Friends* stick together, whether they are men or women," I told him. "And Paige is my friend."

"Sorry. I shouldn't have said that last bit," he said, suddenly smiling gently at me. If it had happened before my time married to Max, it might even have worked, but as it was, I was immune to the charms of overtly handsome men. The inoculation with my ex-husband had certainly been painful enough.

"No, you shouldn't have," I told him.

"But what can I do to get her to listen to me?" he practically begged me as he stood in the middle of the street.

"Respect her wishes and leave her alone," I told him.

"I'm afraid that's the one thing I'm *not* willing to do," the man said.

"Then you've got yourself quite a dilemma, don't you?" I asked him as I got into the Jeep and drove home.

I waited in my vehicle for ten minutes, just in case he decided to follow me home to continue the argument, but finally, I realized he wasn't coming.

Grabbing all three bags of leftovers, it was all that I could do to carry them up onto the porch, but when I saw what was there waiting for me, I dropped the bags out of instinct.

Someone had clearly paid me a visit while I'd been gone.

I knelt down and looked at the object before I moved it from where it leaned against my front door. At first glance, it appeared to be a rudimentary cross made from two sticks bound together at the crosspiece with rough twine. It was something that might mark a pet's grave, but it sent me chills as I picked it up gingerly and threw it out into the side yard. What exactly was it supposed to mean? Was it a warning, a message of another kind, or simply someone's idea of a joke? If the latter had been the intent, it hadn't worked, because I wasn't laughing.

A little more troubled than I had been a few minutes earlier, I picked up the bags from Napoli's and opened the front door.

Before I walked inside, though, I paused, turned, and looked around out into my front yard, which basically led straight into the park.

If anyone was watching me, I couldn't see them, but that didn't mean I couldn't give them a message nonetheless.

"I'm warning you right now that you're messing with the wrong lady." Saying it aloud made me feel better somehow, as though I were taking control of the situation, and not just to reacting to someone else.

I closed the door firmly behind me, locked the cottage up, and decided to put it out of my mind.

After all, I had dessert in that bag, as well as more leftovers than I could have imagined.

It was time to taste the goodies Angelica had packed me.

It was without a doubt the best tiramisu I'd ever had in my life, and that was saying something. I thought about calling Angelica again to thank her for her generosity, but a quick glance at the clock made me realize that though my night was winding down, hers was just beginning in earnest. I'd make it a point to tell her later, but for now, I had some Tupperware to fill and organize.

That was my kind of project, and I found myself smiling as I worked, happy that my friend had shown me how much she cared with one of the most concrete ways there was, by feeding me exquisitely.

I finished the portion of dessert that I'd taken out of the container, and then I turned on an old movie. It was a romantic comedy, no big surprise, the kind of thing I watched when Jake was out of town. It wasn't that he didn't enjoy them too. I just had to trade off an action/adventure for every sappy one I made him watch. He'd opened my horizons since we'd gotten married, and I now enjoyed a little, and I mean little, excitement, but I figured I'd had enough in my normal life that I could use something light when I was trying to relax. I honestly thought "light" entertainment got a bad name. After all, it was cozy and comfortable watching two people make their way through life's obstacles they faced, some of them self-generated, and wondering how they would ever get together in the end but knowing that somehow they would. The world made sense in those movies, and who didn't want a little of that in their lives?

I know I did.

Unfortunately, no matter how good my intentions had been to watch the movie, I fell asleep before those crazy kids found their way to each other in the end.

The next morning, at a little after two-thirty, when the rest of the world was still soundly asleep if they had any sense at all, I woke up and got ready for work. I knew that I'd have to watch the movie over again that night, but that shouldn't be a problem. I wasn't sure when Jake would be back, but I had a feeling that he had his hands full at the moment. That made me miss him even more, and I wanted to call him to tell him how much I loved him, but it would have to wait until a more normal hour. He was easygoing about that kind of thing, but there was no reason to push my luck, and I knew it.

There was a light frost on my Jeep's windshield, and after I scraped it enough to see out of, I drove to the donut shop to get ready for another day.

I was expecting to be alone there, at least until Emma came in an hour later, so I was kind of surprised to see a squad car parked in front of Donut Hearts.

I just hoped that whoever was there wasn't going to bring me some bad news to start my morning.

It was worth wishing for, even though I didn't think I had much of a chance of it coming true.

Chapter 5

"HOW'S MARRIED LIFE treating you?" I asked the chief as I got out my keys. "Don't tell me that you're in Grace's doghouse already."

"What makes you say that?" the chief of police asked as he followed me inside Donut Hearts.

"You're working the graveyard shift," I said. "It doesn't take a rocket scientist to figure out, does it?"

"Darby called in sick again," the chief said. "There was no one else to cover his shift, so I had to do it myself."

"Has he been doing that a lot lately?" I asked as I started flipping on light switches, the coffee urn, and the fryer in back.

"This is the third night this month," Chief Grant said as he stifled a yawn. "I'm putting him on probation if he ever comes to work again."

"What if he's really sick?" I asked. I knew Darby pretty well, and I liked him.

"Then he needs to see a doctor to get it taken care of. What I think is that he's *lovesick*. He met a girl in Hickory, and he's trying to work a full-time job and court her at the same time."

"What's so hard about that? You managed to do it, and so did Jake," I told him.

"Yeah, but we're exceptional as far as most men go," the chief said with a grin.

"That you are," I answered. "So, you didn't come by on more urgent business than looking for a cup of coffee?" A sudden thought, or more specifically a pair of them, occurred to me. "It's not Geneva Swift, is it? Or Richard Covington?"

The chief sat down on the chair I had in my kitchen as I started pulling ingredients, bowls, and other tools out so I could get started on the cake donuts.

"Who exactly are they? Suzanne, have you been making new friends?"

"Hardly," I told him. "Geneva is Momma's new assistant, and we get along like oil and water. As for Richard Covington, he used to be good friends with Paige Hill, and I emphasize 'used to be.'"

"No, neither one of them is in any trouble, at least as far as I know," he replied, but I could see that he was concerned about something.

"Well, as much as I know you enjoy my company, something tells me that you didn't just pop in to say hello. What's on your mind, Chief?"

"Is it really that obvious?" he asked, clearly upset about something.

"It is to me. If you're here for advice about Grace, I'm afraid you've wasted a trip," I told him quickly. "Whatever you're unsure about, just know that I'm on her side. Period. You should apologize."

He looked surprised by the firmness of my declaration. "Honestly? We've been friends for a long time. You wouldn't even *listen* to my side of it before you decided how to react?"

"Grace is the sister I never had," I told him. "Like I said, the only advice I'll give you is general in nature but still very useful. If you're arguing, apologize. If you don't know what you did, but Grace is clearly upset with you anyway, apologize. And if you know without a shadow of doubt that you're right and she's wrong..."

"Let me guess," he interrupted me. "I should apologize." At least he said it with a grin.

"It couldn't hurt," I told him as I started mixing things together in a large bowl.

"Is that really what women want?" he asked me sincerely.

"Of course it isn't, you big idiot," I said as I swatted him with a nearby hand towel. "That's advice for a moron, and Chief, you are many things, but stupid you are not. You should talk to her, Stephen, and find out what's bothering her so you two can work it out together," I said, using his first name instead of his title. That was the kind of conversation we were having, despite the fact that he was in uniform. "Is that why you came by?"

"No, but I'll take your advice anyway. I'm sure that I'll need it before long," he added sheepishly.

"There's no doubt in my mind," I said with a warm smile. "If that wasn't it, then what's going on that's got you so upset in the middle of the night."

"It's the mayor. I'm worried he's leaving April Springs."

"*What?*" I asked as I dropped the spatula in my hand out of shock. "Where is he going? Will it be temporary or permanent? Why would he go? He's got a great job, he's good at it, and he's lived here all of his life. I don't understand," I said as I knelt down, picked up the dropped implement, and put it into the sink. I'd wash it later, or better yet, Emma would when she came in an hour later.

"I don't know the specific answers to *any* of those questions," the chief said.

"Then what's the general one?" I asked.

"He's doing it out of love," Chief Grant said, and suddenly my dinner at Napoli's the night before started to make sense.

"He and Angelica have been having problems lately," I said.

"How did you know that?" the chief asked as I finished mixing the basic cake donut batter with a clean utensil.

"She told me last night," I admitted. "She thinks he's growing distant from her, and she said that he definitely had something on his mind."

"Yeah, well, giving up your career and shaking up your entire life to be with a woman is *something*, all right," the chief said unhappily.

"Need I remind you that Jake did just that for me?" I asked him as I continued working, dividing the batter into different bowls so I could create different-flavored donuts.

"That's different," he said hastily.

"How so? Jake was at the pinnacle of his career when he walked away from it all for love," I reminded him.

"Yeah, well, he had you waiting for him here. Why wouldn't he?"

I shook the spatula at him. "Don't try to flatter me, bub. I've known you too long. If ever there was a woman worth throwing your life away for, it's Angelica DeAngelis."

"Sure, she's a great lady, and an amazing chef to boot, but why can't he commute? He could be with her at night and just be half an hour away from us. A lot of folks drive that much every day without a problem."

"I don't think it's the commute that's the problem," I told him. "I'm sure George doesn't want Angelica to feel neglected. It's taken him a lifetime to find his soulmate, and I'm certain that he doesn't want to lose her."

"Do you think she gave him an ultimatum?" the chief asked me as I started adding specific ingredients to the bowls of batter.

I was folding the blueberries into one when I said, "I can guarantee you that she has no idea he's even thinking about stepping down. If she had, she would have mentioned it to me last night."

"Even something that private?" the police chief asked me.

"Even that," I told him. I was as sure of it as I was of my own first name.

"So she might not even know what he's up to," the chief said, nodding.

"How did *you* find out about it?" I asked, a little miffed that George hadn't discussed the matter with me.

"I happened to see him talking with a real estate agent from Union Square yesterday. They were standing in front of City Hall when I walked by, and the man introduced himself to me as he handed me his business card. George looked pretty embarrassed by the whole thing. After the realtor left, I asked George point-blank what was going on, and he told me."

"I can't believe he just blurted it out like that," I told the chief.

"He kind of swore me to secrecy," the police chief admitted.

"What? And you betrayed that trust? Come on, Chief. What's gotten into you? Can *I* even trust you anymore?"

"Take it easy, Suzanne. I told him there were two women I had to tell, and he might as well get used to the idea," the chief said.

"Grace was one, and I was the other?" I asked him, surprised to be in that inner circle. It felt good having friends who trusted me, and I always tried to earn the respect it implied.

"You're just about the only two women I'm close to these days," the chief admitted a little bit sheepishly. "George is expecting your call this morning, by the way. I wanted reinforcements, and you're the best ally I have in this mess."

"I'm touched," I said sincerely.

"Maybe you shouldn't be," Chief Grant said. "I'm afraid I've dragged you down into the trenches with me. Suzanne, we need to do whatever it takes to convince George to stay as our mayor in April Springs, and I mean anything."

"I agree that George is made for us, but why are you so adamant that he stay?" I asked as I started filling up the donut dropper that was made to take the batter and drop specific amounts into the hot oil.

"If he steps down, you know who's going to take his place?" the chief asked glumly.

"Cora Hartley," I said. "I can see your problem."

"Can you?" he asked me. "She wants to cut my budget in half. To do it, I'd have to fire half my staff when I can't keep good people on as it is, and our ability to keep this town safe will be greatly compromised. I can't, I won't allow that."

It was as strong a speech as I'd ever heard the man give in the entire time I'd known him. "Stephen, are you thinking about running against her to take George's place?"

"What? Don't be ridiculous," the chief said vehemently. "I'd never dream of going into politics. I'm a cop, Suzanne, through and through."

"So was George before he was mayor," I reminded him. "We could do worse than have you as our fearless leader."

"You've been smelling donut fumes too long," he said. "You've gone around the bend. I didn't ask you to run my mayoral campaign, Suzanne. I want you to help me convince George to stay on."

"That's true, but if his mind is made up, what can we really do about it?" I asked him.

"That's just it. I don't think he *wants* to leave us. I think he believes that he *has* to."

"That is a different matter entirely. I'll speak with him," I said as I started fishing donuts out of the oil and putting them on the glazing rack.

"This morning?" he asked me.

"This morning. If I don't see him by the time I close, I'll leave here and track him down as soon as I'm finished for the day. That's the most I can promise," I said.

"Okay then. I'm putting this mess in your hands," the chief said as he stood.

"Thanks. Thanks a lot," I said sarcastically. "Hey, how about a donut and some coffee before you go back out on patrol?" I asked him.

"No, thanks," he said, and then he stopped in his tracks. "You know something? There's no reason in the world that I shouldn't."

"That's my boy," I said with a grin as I pulled a freshly glazed old-fashioned cake donut off of the rack and wrapped it in some parchment paper for him. "Let's get you that coffee too," I said as I pulled the last cake donut from the oil and doused it in glaze.

The police chief never got his coffee, though.

As I was pouring it into a cup for him to take with him, something hit my shop's front window with a boom that made me worry that the glass might shatter under the impact.

When I looked to see what had happened, I saw the bloody hand-print covering part of the word Hearts on my window, and as I rushed to get a better look, I saw a body lying facedown on the sidewalk in front of my shop in the middle of the night.

Chapter 6

THE CHIEF AND I RUSHED outside, and as we knelt down, I saw clothes that could have belonged to any number of men in April Springs. From the man's build alone, it could have been Jake, George Morris, or even one of the many customers who frequented my shop.

At least Jake was still out of town.

I hoped so, anyway.

"There's a pulse, but just barely," the chief said as he radioed for an ambulance and backup.

"Who is it?" I asked him.

"I don't know, and I'm afraid to turn him over until the paramedics get here," he answered.

He searched the body carefully for a wound, and when he got to the back of the man's neck, he pulled away quickly.

From the light filtering out onto the sidewalk from the donut shop, I could see a stain on his hand that hadn't been there before. The police chief shook his head for a moment and then put his hand back where it had been before. "There's a puncture wound there like an ice pick would make," he told me. "Where are those guys?" he asked as he looked down Springs Drive.

"I don't know," I said as the ambulance siren started to wail from a distance. "I heard you calling for backup, but I thought you were the only one on duty tonight," I told him.

"I'm getting some folks out of bed for this," Chief Grant said, and then he looked at me carefully. "I know you want to get some pictures, so go ahead."

"I'm not ghoulish," I protested.

"I'm not saying that you are. I wouldn't mind a record of this, either. Take a bunch, and forward them to me."

I was happy enough to comply. As I took my phone out and started snapping photos, I had to admit that it had been my nature in the past to record scenes like this one whenever they happened, but this was the first time the chief of police had actually encouraged me to do it. Was Chief Grant starting to accept that I had something to bring to the table, or was holding a hand on a man's mortal wound enough to shake him out of his usual thought process?

I didn't care. Either way, I was going to record what I could. I took enough photos of the body to satisfy me, and then I got a few shots of the window as well. The bloody handprint was chilling, especially since I still didn't know who the victim was yet.

The EMTs arrived in their ambulance and quickly took over from the chief. We stood there together and watched them work, checking for a pulse and doing their best to keep the man alive without turning him over.

After a few minutes, one of them shook her head at the other, who flipped the body over.

That was right. It was a body, not a living, breathing person anymore.

My heart stuck in my throat as they did it. I was convinced beyond any doubt that my good friend and our mayor, George Morris, lay dead on the sidewalk in front of my shop.

When I saw the man's face, I'd never been happier to be wrong in my life.

That didn't mean that I was pleased that someone had died at my feet. I was just happy that it hadn't been my old friend.

Paige wasn't going to be nearly as pleased though, I imagined, because the body in question belonged to the man I'd heard her fighting with the day before.

Whatever her beef had been with Richard Covington, the feud was now over, because the man was clearly past caring what anyone thought of him anymore.

"What do you think you're doing?" the chief barked at the EMT.

"We need to move him, don't we?"

"Not if he's expired," he said. "Wait for the coroner."

"Come on, Howie. I *told* you that," the woman paramedic said. *Gert* was on her name tag, and they both looked new to me.

"Sorry," he said, clearly not remorseful at all as they both took a few steps back and waited.

The chief glanced at me. "Who is it, Suzanne? It's pretty clear you recognized him."

"I don't know *everyone* in April Springs," I protested, still wrapping my head around the fact that someone I'd spoken to so recently was now dead. It was never an easy thing to take in, seeing life one second and death the very next one.

"Don't give me that. I saw your face when they flipped him over. You know this guy, so tell me who he is?"

"His name is—was, I guess—Richard Covington," I said, knowing that I couldn't protect Paige by denying that I knew the victim. Not only would Chief Grant find out soon enough, but he would also have a reason to stop trusting me when he did. I'd do whatever I could to help Paige, but that didn't include lying to another friend, let alone the chief of police.

"As in Paige Hill's ex you were telling me about earlier," he said with a frown.

"We don't know for sure that he was her ex anything," I protested.

"But she's the only one in town who knew him, right?" the chief asked.

"I don't know that that's true, either," I said.

"You'd never laid eyes on him yourself until yesterday, though," the chief said.

"That's true, but that doesn't mean that he didn't know anybody else in town."

"Fine. I'll get it from Paige when I speak with her," Chief Grant said.

"It's a quarter till four in the morning," I reminded him. "Isn't there any chance it can wait until she's up?"

"If it was about a parking ticket or something like that, sure, but this is murder. There are no business hours when it comes to homicide. Suzanne, I shouldn't have to remind you of that."

"You don't," I answered. "This just stinks."

"That it does," the chief said as reinforcements arrived, including the "sick" Darby Jones.

"Feeling better?" Chief Grant asked him sarcastically.

"I'm sorry, Boss. It won't happen again. She broke up with me." He looked truly remorseful, but the police chief clearly wasn't buying it.

"We'll discuss that later, but for now, get the forensics kit out of my trunk and start videotaping the scene."

"Yes, sir," Darby said without even glancing in my direction.

The new coroner, a doctor from Maple Hollow, rolled up and got out of her car. Even in scrubs, I could tell that she was an attractive woman, fit and shapely. Looking at her, you'd never know that it was almost four in the morning. She smiled brightly at the police chief, barely glanced at the EMTs, and ignored me altogether, which was fine with me. "I was at the hospital working a shift in the ER," she said.

"Hey, Doc," the police chief told the young attractive doctor.

"Please, I told you before. Call me Zoey, Stephen," she said with an even brighter smile, if that were possible. I had to wonder if Dr. Zoey was aware that our young police chief was a married man, because she looked at him like a hungry man looks at a steak dinner.

"Not on duty, Dr. Hicks," he said with a smile.

"Of course, Chief Grant," she answered with a wink as she knelt by the body.

The doctor pulled on some gloves, did a quick but thorough examination on the spot, and then she pulled the gloves off again in an obviously well-practiced set of motions. "He died less than half an hour ago, either from the puncture wound at the base of his neck or the blunt-force trauma to the back of the skull. Contrary to what you might think, the stab wound didn't kill him instantaneously."

"He wasn't murdered here, though. We *saw* him hit that glass with his hand, and nobody else was here when he did. How did he manage to hold on long enough to get here?" I asked her, not thinking about the appropriateness of my right to question her.

"And you are?" she asked me pointedly.

"Suzanne Hart. I own this shop," I told her.

"She's with me," the police chief said. "You can answer her questions."

Instead of doing that, though, she looked at me again with a much more critical eye. "I thought you worked for a cosmetics company, and someone said that your name was Grace, not Suzanne."

"Grace is his wife *and* my best friend," I explained.

"And yet you're out with the police chief in the middle of the night," she said, more of an accusation than a statement.

"She helps me out from time to time," the chief said. Was he trying to hide a blushing attack? Seriously? "On *some* of my cases. Her husband is a retired state police investigator," he added lamely, as though that made everything all right.

"I see," she said, but did she?

I didn't care. "About the wounds. Why would someone stab him and *then* hit him in the back of the head?"

"If I had to wager a guess, I'd say that the blow to his head knocked him out, and then whoever did it used the ice pick to finish the job. *Maybe* they did it in the reverse order. I honestly couldn't say at this point."

"So it's *also* possible that whoever stabbed him thought he would die instantly, and when he didn't, they decided to finish the job another way," I said.

"That's also within the realm of possibility," she admitted, "but until I can examine the body at the morgue, I can't say for sure." She turned back to the chief and added, "Is that all you needed from me tonight?"

There was more to that offer than the words expressed, and what was more, even Chief Grant recognized it. "That's it. Thanks for coming so quickly."

"For you? Always," she said, and then she left, nodding at the EMTs on her way to her car and still barely acknowledging my presence.

"You can load him up and take him to the hospital morgue now. We've gotten all of the photos and video we need," the chief told the EMTs.

After they did as they were told, a few other officers arrived at the scene, along with my assistant, Emma Blake.

Now I was in for a whole new round of trouble, given that her father, Ray, owned and operated the only paper in the area, the *April Springs Sentinel*.

"What's going on, Suzanne?" Emma asked as she noticed the bloody handprint on the glass. "Are you *okay*?"

"I'm a little shaken up, but other than that, I'm fine. We had an accident this morning." That didn't even begin to cover what had happened to Richard Covington, but it was all that I was willing to say at the time.

"What happened? Did somebody get hit by a car?" she asked as she looked around for a damaged vehicle. "Did they die?" she added softly.

"It wasn't a car accident, but someone did die," I told her. "Let's go inside, and I can tell you about it. Is that okay?"

"Hang on a second," she said as she walked over to Chief Grant, who was busy giving instructions to some of his team. "Chief, got a second?"

"Sorry, but I'm a little busy right now, Emma," he said, trying his best to ignore her.

"That's okay. I'm sure you won't mind if I call my dad," she said as she pulled out her cell phone.

That wouldn't be an ordinary father/daughter conversation. Ray Blake would descend on us like a vulture once he heard the news. I'd tried to at least delay that happening, but the police chief was going to have to help me out some.

"Hang on," he said as he frowned. "I have a second."

"Good," she responded as she put her phone away. "What happened? Who is the victim? What's the cause of death? How was the body discovered? When did it happen—do you know yet?"

"I thought you were a donut maker like Suzanne," the chief said, shaking his head. "I didn't realize you were a reporter too."

"Those are the questions I know Dad's going to ask me," Emma explained. "I thought I'd save you some grief before I called him."

It was clear that Chief Grant was not all that eager to face Ray Blake this early in the morning, or at any time of day, most likely. "If you give me an hour, I'll have a great deal more to tell you."

Emma shook her head. "Sorry, that's not going to work. How about five minutes?"

"I might be able to cut it to half an hour," the chief said.

"Five minutes. It's the best I can do, and I'm going to get in hot water with my father as it is. Come on, Chief. Give me *something.*"

He shrugged. "I wish I could, but we're still gathering evidence."

"At least tell me who it was," she insisted.

"I don't have official confirmation as to the victim's identity," he said, doing his best not to make eye contact with me.

"So he's not from around here," Emma said. "Interesting. Was it the man I saw talking to the mayor in front of City Hall yesterday?"

How had she seen that? I certainly hadn't told her, and I doubted anyone else had, either. Worse yet, I saw the chief flinch a fraction of a second when she asked her question.

"Good, we've confirmed that much. You might as well tell me his name."

"As far as I know, the victim had no contact with the mayor," he said. "I'm sorry, Emma, but I can't say more than that."

"I'm sorry too, Chief, but I have to call my dad," she said as she pulled her phone back out.

"Do what you have to do," he said as he turned to one of his officers. "Clean up that window, and I mean now."

Before he could get out the cleaner and paper towels, though, Emma took a photo with her phone of the bloody handprint.

"It's for Dad," she explained. "He'll want to run it in the paper."

I said, "That's your decision, but do you honestly want folks around here associating murder with Donut Hearts? That handprint makes quite a visual impact, doesn't it?"

Emma looked upset when I pointed that fact out to her. My message was clear. Where did her loyalties lie, with her father or her boss and friend? She could make only one of us happy, and I wasn't entirely sure which one it might be.

After a moment, Emma did something on her phone and then turned to me. "Will you look at that? I accidently erased that shot while I was trying to send it to my father." She then turned to the cop in question, who still hadn't acted. "Officer, if you don't hurry up and clean that window, I might have time to take another picture of it."

"Thanks," I told her. "It could really hurt business if that got out."

She shook her head. "It's going to be bad enough when Dad blasts this all over the front page," she told me. "I can't keep him from running the story, Suzanne. I'm sorry."

"Hey, it's not your fault. We all have enough trouble justifying our own actions, let alone other people's, including our parents," I told her. "At any rate, we need to get to work. I'm afraid this has put me behind, so I won't be getting a break today. Sorry."

"It's fine," she said. As she started inside, she turned back to the chief. "You said one hour?"

He shrugged. "Like I said, let's make it a half hour. Thanks," he answered as he smiled at her.

"You are most welcome," Emma said, setting the alarm on her phone for thirty minutes, no doubt.

Once Emma and I were inside, I got to work on the yeast donuts as she started in on the dishes I'd generated so far. "Okay, just between the two of us, who was it out there who died?" she asked me.

"Do you really want to know?" I asked, trying to protect Paige Hill as long as I could. Once Emma knew Richard's name and his connection with April Springs, I was afraid that my bookstore-owning friend was going to have more than her fair share of negative publicity.

Then again, most likely, so would I.

"Maybe not," she said with a nod. "What I don't know, I can't tell. I do want to know one thing. Did you see it happen?"

"Is this off the record?" I asked her.

"Of course it is. I'm not a reporter," she answered stiffly.

"So, you're telling me that you've *never* shared details of something you've seen with your father?"

"Well, when you put it that way, I suppose I *am* a reporter. I'm not on staff, though, so I guess that makes me a stringer."

"I'll ask you one more time, then. Is this off the record?"

"Yes. I give you my word," Emma said solemnly, and I believed her.

"The chief and I were talking about something entirely different when there was a boom from the front window. The victim nearly put his hand through the glass trying to get our attention or maybe just trying to keep from falling. When we rushed outside, he was still alive, but by the time the paramedics got here, he was gone."

"Was I right in assuming that it was someone new to town?" she asked me. "We're still off the record, so don't worry about me blabbing it to Dad. I honestly just want to know."

"His name was Richard Covington," I said.

"And what's his connection to April Springs?" Emma followed up.

"Are you *sure* you're not a reporter?" I asked her.

"I'm sure. I'm just nosy, that's all," she answered with a slight grin.

"Isn't that the same thing?" I wondered aloud.

"Part of it, anyway. You didn't answer my question."

"Imagine that," I told her with a smile of my own.

"Does that mean you don't know or you just aren't telling me?" Emma pressed.

"I don't think it's going to snow today, but you never know. I understand we're getting a cold front this evening that might drop the temperature below freezing."

Emma shook her head, but I could still see her smile. "Whenever you give me the weather report unsolicited, you're not going to answer my real questions, are you?"

I pretended not to hear her as I finished measuring out the ingredients for the yeast donuts and let them mix together in the stand mixer. After everything was incorporated, I took the dough hook off and covered the top of the mixer bowl with plastic wrap. That would normally be when we took our break, but I'd used that time up talking to the chief outside. While the dough was going through its first proof, I started carrying trays of cake donuts out front to the display cases. If I happened to get a peek at what was going on outside, so much the better.

The police force, for what it was worth, was still out there, working the crime scene, and I looked out into the park and saw someone's flashlight bobbing up and down as though they were following a trail of some sort.

I had a hunch I knew what kind of lead it was too.

Unless I missed my guess, it was most likely a trail of blood.

Chapter 7

I WAS ABOUT TO GO BACK into the kitchen when I heard Emma's alarm go off, set to remind her when it was time to call her father.

Ready or not, the police were about to get an unwelcome visit from what counted as the press in our little town.

Emma walked past me as she started to make her call. "Suzanne, do you mind if I take my break, anyway?" she asked.

"Of course not," I said. "I might even get a minute or two myself once I get these donuts trayed and in the cases."

"I can help," Emma offered, putting away her phone as she spoke.

"No, you respected the chief's wishes. Go on, make that call." I wasn't a big fan of Ray Blake's, but I loved his daughter as though she were my own, so I wasn't about to stand in her way.

"Thanks. You're the best," she said with a grin as she pulled her phone back out and headed out the door.

"Don't I know it," I said with a smile of my own, "but it's always nice when other people realize it too."

She was laughing as she walked out, which was a good sound given what had already happened this morning.

That was when I realized that I had a call of my own to make.

I should have done it before, but I suppose the shock of finding Richard Covington's body in front of my shop had made me a bit scattered.

Paige needed to know what had happened, and if I could tell her before the police made it over there, so much the better.

I failed at it, though. She answered on the second ring. "Sorry, I can't talk. The police chief is sitting in my living room." I heard someone say something from far away, and she added, "Chief Grant said to tell you hello."

"I'm sorry, Paige. I should have called you earlier."

"No worries, Suzanne. Listen, I've got to go. I'll come by the shop later, and we can catch up. Is that okay?"

"That's fine, but stay strong, and don't say anything you don't want to say. If you need the name of a good lawyer, I can hook you up," I told her.

"I appreciate that, but I don't need one. I didn't do anything wrong."

I was about to tell her that it wasn't necessarily relevant when she hung up on me.

It was out of my hands at that point.

I just hoped that my delay in getting in touch with her hadn't cost her anything but time.

I finished working and joined Emma at our table outside, though the temperature had already fallen since I'd come into the shop. We might be in for some wintery weather after all. "Did you get ahold of him?" I asked as I took my seat.

"He's on his way," she answered. "I don't want to sabotage things here, but we both know that he was going to find out sooner or later."

"I understand that," I told her. "I was hoping for later, but I can't blame you a bit. I'm just happy you deleted that photo."

"Yeah, that was stupid of me," she said.

I wasn't about to admit that I'd done the same thing and that I'd taken the exact same photograph myself. In my defense, I'd done it at the behest of the police chief, but if that image got out, it could do me more damage than a thousand words. The bloody imagery was way too powerful for my taste.

"How long do you think it will take him to get here?" I asked as I glanced at my watch. I was an old-fashioned kind of gal in some ways. I liked the feel of a watch on my wrist. Part of that was that I hated to have to pull my phone out every instance I wanted to know the time.

"Three minutes, maybe four if he stops, or even slows down, for the stop sign at the end of our street," she said.

"Isn't he afraid of getting a ticket?" I asked her.

"Before five in the morning, when he's racing for a story? I doubt it would bother him one bit. Shoot, knowing Dad, he would probably revel in it."

"He probably would at that," I said as my handheld alarm went off much too soon. "That's it for me, but if you want to hang around out here and wait for your dad, I'm okay with that."

"I shouldn't," she said, not moving from her seat.

"Hey, I get it. He's your father." As I unlocked the front door, I added, "Just one thing. You are welcome inside the shop before we open. Just you."

"I understand," she said, and I knew that she did, even though I'd felt the need to remind her.

"I'll see you soon, then."

"Not if I see you first," she answered happily.

I rolled my eyes at her, but I couldn't bite down my smile entirely.

Emma was a little crazy, but she was my kind of crazy, so that was fine with me.

Her father, on the other hand, was a completely different matter altogether, and I didn't want to have to speak with him until later, if it was at all possible.

And since Donut Hearts was mine and no one else's, nobody came in unless I invited them.

No one.

Emma came back into the shop ten minutes later, obviously troubled by something.

"No," I said before she could say a word. "I won't let your father interview me for the newspaper, not now, and not ever," I said as I continued to work on the yeast dough.

"How did you know that was what I was going to ask you?"

"It's not exactly a guess based on your father's history," I told her.

"There's just one thing, though. He said that if you don't talk to him now, he's going to come when we open and pester you in front of our customers until you give him something he can use." She took a deep breath and then added, "I'm just the messenger, so don't shoot me, okay?"

"I'll try not to, but it's going to be tough," I told her, and then I added a slight smile to show that I wasn't completely serious, just about eighty-five percent.

"I knew better than to bring this to you, but we both know how persistent my father can be," she apologized.

"You know what? You're right. I'll be right back," I said as I washed my hands.

"Do you want me to come with you?" Emma offered.

"That depends. Do you want to get your own father's blood on you?" I asked her, a grim determination to end this once and for all pulsing through me.

"No, thanks. I've got so many dishes to do there's just no time. Sorry," she said without a hint of remorse in her voice.

"No problem," I told her.

Ray was looking awfully smug as he saw me come toward the door. Wow, was that not going to last.

"I hate to use the force of the press, Suzanne, but I'm glad you were able to see that this is in your best interests."

Instead of answering him, I turned to Darby Jones, who was just finishing up with his equipment. "Officer, would you please escort this man off my property?"

Ray smiled wickedly. "Sorry, but this is public space in front of your shop."

"Not all of it," I said as I pointed to the sidewalk. "*That's* where the line of demarcation is."

"Did you kill that man, Suzanne, or are you just covering for whoever did?" Ray asked me.

He could tell the moment he said it that he'd crossed a line that couldn't be uncrossed.

I turned to Darby Jones, who was a regular customer of mine, and said, "Do me a favor and shoot him if he trespasses again."

"You know I can't do that," he said, and then he added with a grin, "but if he were disturbing the peace and resisting arrest, we might have a case for the use of deadly force."

Ray looked from the cop to me, hoping to see a smile, which he didn't. "You know you have to talk to me sooner or later."

"There we disagree," I told him. "You are not getting a quote from me now or ever again, Ray. I've had enough of your attempts to bully me and browbeat me into cooperating with you. In the past, I've been nice to you out of deference to your wife and daughter, but you've gone too far this time. Take my advice and go while you're just a little bit behind."

"I'll leave," he said, "but you should know that Emma and Sharon won't be working for you anymore."

Again, the man's mouth kept digging him deeper and deeper into trouble.

"Let's find out, shall we?" I pulled out my phone and called Sharon Blake. "Sharon? Sorry it's so early, but when I refused to give your husband a quote after he accused me of murder, he told me that you weren't ever going to work at Donut Hearts again. Is that true?"

"Put him on the phone," Sharon said icily. "No, this might take a while. I'm hanging up so I can call him myself."

"Does that mean you're still going to work for me?" I asked her just to be sure.

"I may be divorced, but I'll still be at Donut Hearts as long as you'll have me, and so will Emma," she said, and then she hung up.

"You were bluffing. You didn't call her," Ray said as his phone began to ring.

"You might want to get that," I told him, offering him the first and maybe the last smile he would get from me that day, or ever. "It's for you."

I left him outside and winked at Officer Jones on my way in. He saluted me with two fingers to the brim of his hat, and I headed back inside.

"Your father just accused me of murder," I told Emma. "When I told him I was finished with him, he said that you and your mother were quitting Donut Hearts."

"He didn't!"

"Oh yes he did. Officer Jones heard it if you don't believe me. I called your mother, and she told me it wasn't true, so now I'm asking you. I won't hold it against you if you decide to back your father, but I won't have this hanging over my head. Emma, are you in, or are you out?"

"I'm in," she said as she dried her hands. "Wait until I get through with him. He won't know what hit him."

I put a light hand on her shoulder. I wasn't sure that I'd ever seen her so angry. "You might want to do that later. When I left him, your mother was giving him a pretty good beating from the sound of it."

"It's nothing like what he's going to get from me. I'm sorry, Suzanne. I don't know what else I can say."

I hugged her. "You don't have to say anything. Let's get back to work, shall we?"

"We shall," she said.

We both tried to ease the tension we were feeling in the kitchen as we worked to get ready for our day, but there was an uneasiness there, and we both obviously felt it.

At six a.m. on the dot, I went out to open the front door.

Ray was standing there with flowers and a look of contrition on his face. That may have worked before, but it wasn't going to do him any good now. "Go away, Ray."

"I'm sorry, Suzanne. I got caught up in the heat of the moment."

"I won't tell you again. You're not welcome here."

"Dad, you need to go," Emma said from behind me.

"You're taking *her* side, just like your *mother*?" Ray asked her, incredulous about the mutiny he had on his hands.

"Suzanne won't have you thrown out," Emma said. I was about to protest that was exactly what I was going to do when she added, "I won't let her. That's my job."

Her words stung him as he turned to go, the flowers dropping from his hand. I almost felt sorry for him.

Almost.

Once he was gone, Emma shook her head. "He wants to be an award-winning journalist so badly that he loses touch with reality sometimes." She must have realized how that had sounded, because she quickly added, "Don't get me wrong. I'm not making excuses for him."

"I understand," I told her as my cell phone rang. Could it be Jake, calling to wish me a good morning?

No, but it was certainly unexpected nonetheless given what had gone on a few hours earlier.

It was Paige Hill.

Chapter 8

"ARE YOU OKAY?" I ASKED softly, being careful not to use Paige's name. After all, there was no reason to put any temptation in front of Emma, no matter how angry she might be with her father at the moment.

"No, not really," she said. "Could you possibly let me in the back? I really need a friend right now, and you've been nominated."

"I accept," I told her. "How soon can you get here?"

"Two minutes. I just got out of the police station. The chief decided to finish questioning me there."

"That must have been horrible for you," I told her.

"It was, on a great many levels. I'll see you soon."

"Okay," I said as I put my phone away. There were a few folks outside waiting to get in, no doubt wanting to see where Richard Covington had breathed his last. Though he wasn't a local, that didn't deter the looky-loos from coming out in full force. Sometimes the ghoulish nature of people depressed me just about more than I could stand.

"I need you to take the front and open the shop," I told Emma. "There's something I need to take care of."

"Happy to do it," she said, clearly expecting me to walk out the front door after I unlocked it for our customers.

"I'll be in back, but unless it's an emergency, and I mean a dire one, stay out here. Do you understand?"

Clearly she didn't, but she wasn't about to dispute my directions, given the morning we'd had. "I get it. Take your time, Suzanne."

"Thanks," I said as I walked in back. "You can let them in after I've locked this door."

She nodded, and I did as I'd told her. There were windows in the door to the kitchen, but I knew exactly where Paige and I could stand and not be seen from the dining area of the shop. There were times when I had visitors there who didn't want their presence known to the general public, and this was certainly one of them.

I walked through the kitchen to the back door and opened it for my friend.

Paige was the least put together I'd ever seen her. She was wearing sweats and an old jacket, her makeup was nonexistent, and from the look of her eyes, she'd clearly been crying.

Before she could say a word, I wrapped her in my arms and gave her a hug that told her volumes without saying a word. She seemed to melt into me, and I could feel some of the tension drain from her after a minute.

Paige finally pulled away and asked me, "How did you know I needed that so badly?"

"I just put myself in your shoes," I said. "I have coffee and donuts."

"I'm not hungry," she protested as she sat in the chair.

"You need something in your stomach. Force yourself," I told her as I grabbed an old-fashioned donut from the tray of overflows and poured her a cup of coffee.

She took a small nibble of the donut, then another, and then a third. When she finished it, I was waiting with its replacement.

"I really shouldn't," Paige said, looking at my offering the entire time.

"If you can't indulge yourself right now, when can you?" I asked her.

She didn't need any more persuading.

Once the second treat was gone, I offered her a third. "No, I'm good, but you were right. That was amazing. I can't believe this nightmare is actually happening."

"I'm not going to force you, but if you'd like to talk about it, I'm here for you."

"It's more than that, Suzanne. I need you to prove that I didn't kill Richard Covington."

Chapter 9

"SURELY THE CHIEF DOESN'T honestly think you did it," I told her.

"I wouldn't say that's true, and I'm not sure that I don't blame him," Paige admitted. "After all, who else in town even knew Richard Covington but me?"

"We're not *that* isolated," I told her. "Where is he...was he from originally?"

"Maple Hollow," she said.

"That's not far at all," I told her with obvious relief.

"Why is that such good news?" she asked me.

"He *could* have been from *anywhere*. If you'd told me he was from Colorado or Alaska, then we might have a bigger problem, but Maple Hollow is not that far away."

"Who would want him dead, though?" she asked. "Besides me, I mean." Paige must have instantly realized how that had sounded. "Not that I wanted him dead. It's just that we have a history."

"What happened? Did he break your heart, Paige?" I asked, remembering how betrayed I had felt when Max had slept with another woman while we'd been married.

"No! We never even dated. Richard and I lived beside each other for six years when we were kids," she said. "He was more like a brother than a potential romantic interest for me, no matter how hard he tried to convince me otherwise."

"He was a good-looking guy," I admitted, remembering Rita's comparison of him to Mr. Darcy.

"Maybe, but I never saw him that way."

I believed her. "So, if he didn't cheat on you, what did he do?"

"He stole my grandfather's gold piece," she said. "I knew that he did it, but I could never prove it."

"Was it just sentimental, or was it valuable?" I asked her.

"It was a twenty-dollar Liberty double eagle," she said. "But more than that, it was his good-luck piece, so that made it valuable to me."

"What do you think it was worth?" I asked her.

"Maybe a couple of grand," she said. "I know that might not be much to some folks, but it was a fortune to us back then."

"It *still* sounds like a fortune to me," I said, thinking about how long it would take me to clear two thousand dollars at the donut shop after expenses. "When did all of this happen?"

"Just before we moved," she said. "He and his dad were helping us pack, and the coin suddenly disappeared. Richard denied it, but I *knew* that he took it. After that, I cut him out of my life. When he showed up again yesterday, I hadn't seen him for a good ten years."

"He seemed really adamant about making amends with you," I told her gently.

"His folks died recently," she explained. "I heard it from one of my relatives. Apparently Richard was just about all alone in the world. That's the only reason I can think of that he'd come looking for me again after all of these years."

"Did you see him again last night after he left the bookstore steps?" I asked her.

"No," she said, suddenly avoiding eye contact.

"Paige, how can I help you if you lie to me?" I hated pressing my friend, but what choice did I have? She'd asked for my help, and that meant taking the good and the bad that came with it.

"Fine. He came by my place late last night, but I wouldn't let him in!" she nearly shouted.

"You need to keep your voice down," I said softly. "Especially if you don't want to advertise the fact that you're here. What did he say?"

"He told me that he was staying with an old friend in Maple Hollow, a guy named Rudy Francis. Richard said that he wouldn't leave the area until I'd talk to him, but I told him to leave me alone. Suzanne,

I wouldn't hear him out, and now I can't take it back! What if I was wrong? What if he *didn't* steal that coin? I won't ever be able to forgive myself if that was what happened."

"I get that, but you can't be so hard on yourself. You were just a kid," I told her. "I can't make you any promises, but I'll do everything in my power to help you figure out what happened to him."

"Do you need help? I can turn the bookstore over to Rita," she suggested.

"As much as I appreciate it, I'm not sure this is a case you need to be working on. Folks know you have ties to the victim and that you spent a few hours being interviewed with the chief of police this morning at the station. It might make it difficult for them to open up in front of you."

"In other words, I'd be more of a liability than an asset," she said.

"Yes, that's another way of putting it," I admitted.

"Thank you, Suzanne."

"For digging into this?" I asked her. "You're my friend. I'd do anything for you."

"Yes, that, but also for telling me the truth, even though I lied to you a few minutes ago. It won't happen again. You deserve the complete and utter truth, no matter how bad it might make me look."

"That's all I can ask," I told her.

"If I *can* do anything, let me know," she said as she started for the door.

"Are you going to open the bookstore this morning?" I asked her.

"I hadn't thought about it. Why, should I not? Won't that make me look guilty?"

"It might, but then again, if you're open, folks are going to try to drag things out of you that you might not want to share," I told her.

"Then again, if I lock up, I won't have a chance to defend myself," she answered. "I'm not hiding and hoping this all blows away. I didn't do anything wrong, and I'm not going to act as though I did."

I smiled and patted her shoulder lightly. "The truth is that I'd probably do the same thing in your shoes. In fact, I have," I admitted.

"*You* were accused of murder?" she asked me, clearly surprised by my admission.

"It was before you came to April Springs, but yes, I was. I got through it, though, and so will you."

"With you on my side, I don't have any doubt about it," she answered.

I didn't know quite what to say to her blind show of faith, so all I could do was nod.

Once she was safely out the back, I walked up front to relieve Emma, only to find the donut shop crawling with folks.

None of them seemed all that interested in the donuts or coffee, either.

"We sell donuts here, not answer questions," Emma said a bit impatiently as folks started shouting questions at me the second I walked out.

"You owe us," Nick Williams said.

"Come on. We have a right to know," Wilson Strong added.

"Unless you're hiding something," Marla Humphries piped up.

"Settle down, everybody," I told them, and then I said softly to Emma, "You can go on back into the kitchen. I've got this."

"You're kidding, right? You don't want reinforcements to deal with this mob?" She wasn't exactly quiet as she said it, and there were a few grumbles from the crowd, but I noticed that nobody left, either.

"It's fine. Go finish up those dishes," I instructed her.

"Okay, if you're sure."

"I'm positive," I said.

Once Emma was gone, I turned to the group standing around the counter and put on my best plastic smile. "Okay, who's first?"

"Did you know the guy that got himself killed in front of the shop?" Marla asked snarkily. "Was he an old beau of yours or something?"

"I'm sorry, I didn't make myself clear. Who's first in line to buy donuts?"

There were a great many shrugs, and no one stepped up. That gave me an idea. "I'll make a deal with you. You can ask me anything you'd like, but it's going to cost you a dozen donuts."

"That's not fair," Wilson said. "What am I going to do with a dozen donuts?"

"You could always shove them in that pie hole of yours," Nick said.

"You should talk. What do you weigh, three hundred pounds?" Wilson asked him meanly.

He must have been close to the mark, because Nick blanched a bit. "Not even close," he said.

I had a hunch he was a *little* close.

"Come on. I don't have all day," I told them. "If you're not here to buy donuts or coffee, then you're just blocking the way for my real customers."

"I'll take a dozen; you pick the kind," Nick said, shooting a dirty look toward Wilson, who didn't say a word in reply. No doubt he wanted to hear what was coming next.

After taking Nick's money, I said, "Go on. Ask your question."

"Was he an old boyfriend of yours?" Nick asked.

"Are you really wasting your question on that?" Wilson asked derisively.

"Shut up," Nick said, and then he turned back to me. "Well?"

"No," I answered. "Who's next?"

Nick took his donuts and looked a bit remorseful about how he'd used his question. "Okay, I've got another one."

"One dozen, one question," I reminded him.

He slapped another bill on the counter. "Did you know the guy who got murdered?"

"We'd met," I said. "Next?"

"That's all you're going to say? Come on, Suzanne," Nick protested. "That's like seven bucks a word."

"Don't forget, you got two dozen donuts too," I reminded him.

"Fine," he said as he grabbed the boxes and moved to one side. I noticed that he was in no hurry to leave the shop, which was okay with me. At the rate we were going, I'd be out of donuts before seven, which would certainly free up my day if I chose not to make more. Then I realized that I'd be disappointing my usual customers if I kept this up.

"There's a new policy in place, starting immediately," I announced. "A regular donut will cost you a dollar. If you want a question answered with it, it will be ten."

"That's not fair," Wilson said. "Nick got two dozen with his money."

"Hey, you snooze, you lose," Nick told him, smiling gleefully and obviously glad that he'd made the deal with me early, despite how he'd been disappointed with my answers.

"I'll take one," Marla said. Once we made the transaction, she asked, "Do you know who the police suspect?"

"Yes," I said. "Next?"

"Who is it?" she asked insistently.

"One question, one donut, ten bucks," I reminded her.

"Fine," she said as she slapped another bill down on the counter, a bit more angrily than she needed to, at least as far as I was concerned.

"Who do the police suspect in the murder?" she asked me smugly.

If I answered that, Paige was going to be inundated with her own round of questions sooner than she should be, so I decided on my answer.

"No comment."

"That's not an answer," Marla protested.

"It might not be the answer you were looking for, but it's an answer just the same."

"You promised us answers for our money," she insisted.

"I promised you the right to ask the question. I never said a word about my answers," I said with a bright smile that was real this time.

"What a rip-off. I'm leaving," she said as she walked out the door with her two donuts in hand.

The profit margin on those had been through the roof, but I hadn't done it to make money. Making a point had been much more important.

Several other folks left as well, but a few hung around.

Jackson Boles approached the counter. "What's your question, Jackson?" I asked him.

He grinned at me. "Are you kidding? At that price, who can afford one? No thank you. I'll take two glazed donuts and a small black coffee, and you keep your answers to yourself as far as I'm concerned."

"Here you go," I said as I filled his order.

"You didn't charge me anything," he said, looking confused.

"That's okay. The next few donuts will be on the house. Or should I say courtesy of my previous customers?" I just couldn't pocket that money I'd made answering questions with a clear conscience.

"In that case, I'll take two dozen to go," Jackson said with a grin.

"Two donuts per customer for the next ten customers," I said. "Nice try, though."

"Hey, no harm in asking," he replied happily.

I ended up giving donuts and coffee away to the next twelve folks, which were all that had stuck around after the mob had left. Maybe some of the folks who didn't like the way I did business were right. I wasn't exactly the shrewdest businesswoman on the planet, but I could sleep just fine at night, and that was okay with me, even if I lost money now and then.

Chapter 10

"SUZANNE, I JUST HEARD about what happened," Momma said as she rushed into the donut shop. "That must have been dreadful for you."

"It wasn't all that pleasant, but at least Chief Grant was here with me. It would have been ten times worse if I'd been alone. It's sweet of you to come by and check on me."

"Always," my mother said, though she was obviously still concerned about something.

"Momma, is something wrong?"

"I can't seem to locate Geneva," she said. "After the scolding I gave her yesterday, I'm afraid that she's quit on me."

"I'm so sorry," I said, meaning it. "I didn't mean to run her off."

"You didn't," she said. "She's clearly intimidated by you."

I did a double take. "Me? I don't think so. You should have seen the way she waltzed into the shop yesterday demanding that I sign those franchising papers without even reading them. There is no way that she's afraid of me."

"Suzanne, some folks push hard when they're frightened," Momma told me.

"Then she must have been scared to death of me," I said in wonder.

"If you haven't seen her since she was here yesterday, I'm not sure where to look next."

"I didn't quite say that," I told Momma. "As a matter of fact, I saw her last night at Napoli's. Paige Hill and I went out to dinner, and we saw Geneva getting into a pickup truck as we were arriving."

"Really? Who was she with?"

"I couldn't tell," I admitted.

"I didn't realize she was seeing anyone, but she grew up in Maple Hollow, so I suppose it's possible she reconnected with an old friend when she moved back into the area," Momma said.

"Maple Hollow? Really?" I asked.

"Yes. Why are you suddenly interested in where my assistant is from?" she asked me.

Lowering my voice, I said, "Richard Covington, the man who died right out there, was from Maple Hollow."

"So are thousands of other people," Momma reminded me, unable or uninterested in taking the scolding tone out of her voice. "That doesn't necessarily mean they knew each other."

"They were about the same age," I said, "so it doesn't necessarily mean that they didn't, either."

"Fine. I'll ask her about it if she ever bothers showing up. I just hope it wasn't Baxter you saw her with," Momma said.

"Who's Baxter?" I asked.

"He's the young man who broke her heart and left her at the altar six months ago," Momma said. "Apparently the man was bad news all the way around, from what I've gathered, and if she's taken up with him again, I know that she'll regret it," Momma explained as her telephone rang. "What do you know? It's Geneva."

"Take it here," I said. "I want to know where she's been too."

"Suzanne, honestly," Momma said as she moved toward the front door. "Yes?" she asked, and then she was gone before I could hear anything else.

I wanted to follow her outside, but I couldn't desert my post at the counter without calling Emma up first, and besides, Momma would be none too happy with me if I started eavesdropping on her so blatantly.

I waited on a few more customers, always keeping one eye on my mother, who was standing in front of the shop, talking. To my surprise, she came back in after she hung up, and after I was finished with the two customers I'd been waiting on, she approached the counter. "She admits that she knew him, not well, but still, I thought you should know."

"Where was she this morning?" I asked.

"She claims the alarm on her phone failed to wake her," Momma said severely.

"Did you fire her?"

"Suzanne, I don't terminate employees for one mistake."

"Even if it's a whopper?" I asked her.

She chose not to answer that, which wasn't all that unusual for her when it came to my questions. Instead, she said, "She promised me that she's going to buy three alarm clocks when she's finished with work for the day. I told her that two would be fine, but she insisted."

"Well, I'm glad that's settled," I said.

"As am I," Momma answered. "Try to stay out of trouble for the rest of the day, Suzanne. Would you do that for your mother?"

"I could make you that promise, but I know how upset you get when I lie to you," I told her with a grin. "I love you, Momma."

"I love you too," she answered as she walked out the door.

"Because of?" I asked her, grinning.

"In spite of," she replied, and I got the laugh I'd been looking for.

I needed to check with Paige to see if Geneva had told Momma the truth about how well she'd known the murder victim. It wasn't as though I was hoping that she'd lied to my mother, but I needed to find out one way or the other.

"Paige, do you have a second?" I asked as she answered on the eighth ring.

"I'm kind of busy here right now," she said, the frantic tone telling me all that I needed to know. Evidently, the gossips had uncovered her connection to the murder victim despite my best efforts to keep it a secret.

"Make them buy a book for every question they ask," I suggested.

"What? Isn't that extortion?"

"I'm sure that some folks might see it that way. Why, is that a problem?" I asked her.

"No, maybe not. I'm just not sure I want to answer the kind of questions they might ask me," she admitted.

"Who said anything about you being obligated to answer them?" I asked her.

Paige must have heard the smile in my voice. "Suzanne, you are evil and wicked and brilliant, and I'm proud to call you my friend."

"Right back at you," I said. "Call me back when you get a chance."

"I will, and I have a hunch it's not going to be long."

After she hung up, I waited on a few more customers and did a little cleaning out front when things got slow. It always amazed me how wiping down the tables and gathering the dirty plates and mugs together made me feel so much better about Donut Hearts. Not only did it give folks a better impression of the shop, but it gave me a boost too.

I was just taking a bin of dirty dishes back to Emma when my cell phone rang.

"Want me to cover the front while you take that?" my assistant asked me as I set the tub down near the sink.

"No, I can handle both," I said when I saw that it was Paige.

Wow, that was even quicker than I'd expected.

"I hope you sold lots of books," I told Paige.

"I moved six of them from the bargain table," she answered. "Then they got wise to the fact that I wasn't exactly telling them what they wanted to know, and they ended up leaving."

"I didn't mean to run off your customers," I said, suddenly wondering if my advice had been a little too restrictive for her business.

"Are you kidding? None of them had ever set foot in the bookstore before. Shoot, I may have even made a few converts," she added. "What did you want to talk about?"

"I'm not sure now. Do I have to buy a book first?" I asked her with a laugh.

"For you, they're on the house."

"The books or the questions?" I asked.

"The questions. Sorry for the confusion," she apologized.

"Hey, I have no problem paying for the books I read," I told her. "Do you have any idea if Richard ever dated Geneva Swift? You didn't say anything about it last night, but you mentioned that the two of you had already met. Was that in April Springs?"

"Didn't I say? She went to high school with us for two years," Paige explained. "Yeah, she dated Richard for a few months. He broke up with her when he found out she was moving away. Richard was never a big fan of long-distance relationships, and they weren't exactly hot and heavy, no matter how much Geneva might have wished otherwise. Why, did she say something to you this morning when you apologized to her?"

"I was going to do that first thing, honestly I was, but she never showed up for work," I said.

"So you haven't spoken to her," Paige asked me.

"Not yet, but I'll tell her that I'm sorry the very next time I see her," I promised.

"Listen, a customer just came in who appears to actually be looking for a book. I've got to go," Paige said quickly.

"One more quick question," I asked.

"Okay, but make it fast," she said.

"Could that have been Richard driving the pickup last night that we saw Geneva getting into?"

She hesitated much longer than I would have expected her to before she answered.

"Maybe. He always did love pickup trucks. Now I really have to go. Later."

"I'll talk to you soon," I told her as I hung up.

What had seemed simple at the time was getting more complicated by the minute. Was it possible that Geneva had tried to rekindle the flame with Richard Covington and he'd balked at the notion? If she was as passionate as some folks seemed to think, she could have killed him out of anger over the rejection. It was as good a theory as any, and the next chance I got, I was going to have to ask her about it.

But that was going to have to wait.

At the moment, I still had a donut shop to run.

"Mr. Mayor, just the person I wanted to talk to," I told George Morris as he walked into Donut Hearts ten minutes before we were set to close. "If you hadn't come by, I was going to come looking for you."

"That's never good for me, is it?" George asked. "Sorry I didn't get over here sooner. I heard about what happened this morning. Are you digging into it?"

"Maybe," I said, "but that wasn't what I wanted to discuss with you."

He must have sensed something in my tone. "That blasted police chief can't keep his mouth shut, can he?"

"He warned you that he was going to tell me. Besides, he was concerned, and truth be told, so am I," I told him. There were two customers dawdling over their coffee, having finished their donuts earlier. "Hang on one second."

I walked over to their table. "We're closing early today."

"Hey, I'm not finished with my coffee," Simon Blackstone said in protest as Neddy Jackson got up to go.

"I'll make you one to go," I answered. "You want one too, Neddy?"

"Nope, I'll be floating the rest of the day if I do. See you tomorrow, Suzanne."

"See you," I said.

Simon didn't budge. "What if I wanted another donut too?" he asked.

"Do you?"

"That depends. I heard you were giving them away this morning, so I've been hanging around, hoping you do it again."

"I wasn't giving anything away," I corrected him. "That was because of something else entirely. Besides, you've got money, and don't try to deny it. Why would you waste your morning hoping for a handout?"

"You know how rich people stay rich?" he asked me with a grin. "They don't spend what they have on things they can get for free."

"Fine," I said, grabbing a peach donut I'd tried that morning. It was good enough to sell, though just barely, and I'd actually discouraged a few of my regulars from trying them.

"What is this?" he asked me as I handed him the bag.

"Peach," I said.

He made a face. "I hate peach."

"Hey, don't be a choosy beggar. Do you want it or not?" I asked him. "Either way, it's time to go."

"I guess I'll take it," he said with a grumble.

"Aren't you forgetting something?" I asked him with a plastered-on smile.

"Are you actually expecting a tip?" he asked me with clear disdain.

"From you? No chance, but you could say thank you."

"Thanks, I guess," he said reluctantly. "See you, George," he added to the mayor as he left.

"Good-bye, Simon," George replied a little stiffly.

Once he was gone, I flipped the sign to CLOSED and locked the door.

"Wow, that man is so tight he squeaks when he walks," George said.

"He's harmless enough," I said, not allowing myself to get distracted. "One more second," I said as I walked in back to find Emma sweeping the floor.

"Why don't you take off early? I know you have a lot on your plate right now," I told her.

"Are you sure?" she asked then quickly added, "Strike that. Thank you. That's what I meant to say."

I grinned at her. "You're welcome." I didn't want her going out the front and seeing George Morris there. There was no reason to get her or her father curious about the conversation I was about to have. "Would you mind grabbing the trash and putting it out back on your way out? I'll lock the door behind you."

"Done and done," Emma said, not suspecting what I was up to or not caring, just happy to be getting out of Donut Hearts a little early.

Once I'd locked up behind her, I returned to the front to find the mayor eating a donut and drinking a cup of coffee. "I could make you some fresh if you'd like."

"Donuts or coffee?" he asked with a smile.

"Coffee," I answered. "Neither one of us has time to wait for me to make donuts. Now stop trying to distract me. Why do you want to leave us? Don't you love us anymore?"

George scowled a bit before he answered. "Suzanne, that's not fair, and you know it. I have every right to be happy. You are, so why shouldn't I be?"

I poured myself some coffee, and against my better judgment, I grabbed a donut as well. After all, I had to keep George company, didn't I?

"I didn't realize you were so miserable here," I told him.

"I'm not. It's just that there are other things I'd like to do before I get too old to do them," the mayor told me.

"Tell me this isn't about Angelica," I said.

He looked at me abruptly. "What about her? Did she say something to you?"

I debated keeping my conversation with my friend private, but I quickly decided that this all needed to get out into the open. When things stayed in the shadows, decisions were made that could be regretted later on. George needed to hear what was on his girlfriend's mind.

I just hoped that Angelica could find it in her heart to forgive me.

"She said she was worried that you were pulling away from her. George, are you going to dump her?"

"What? Are you nuts? She's the best thing that's ever happened to me. On the contrary, I'm planning to leave my job and my home and move to Union Square to be closer to her," he said, the words tumbling out of his mouth.

"Does *she* know that?" I asked him. Before he could answer, I said, "No, of course she doesn't. What makes you think she *wants* you to give everything up for her? You're only half an hour away as things stand now."

"That's true, but something's always coming up in my job to keep me from her, and I know she's getting tired of being second on my list of priorities. Anyway, I've been mayor quite a while." After a moment he added thoughtfully, "There would have to be a special election to fill my seat. You could run yourself, Suzanne."

"Have you lost your mind?" I asked, my filter completely gone. "That's the craziest thing I've ever heard in my life. I'm a donut maker, not a politician."

"I was a retired cop when I got the job, remember?" he asked me. "You would make a fine mayor. I'll even campaign for you and give you my endorsement too."

"Stop. Just stop," I said. "I don't want the job, and even if I got it, I'd be terrible at it."

I had no hesitation saying that. George had learned patience in his time as mayor, but I knew that I'd end up alienating half the town my first week in office. Besides, if I was mayor, I'd have to give up too many things, like my privacy for one.

"*Somebody's* got to do it," George said. "Why shouldn't it be you?"

"Because *you're* the only mayor I want for April Springs," I told him sincerely. "George, we need you."

"Well, as nice as that sounds, I have needs too."

He clearly wasn't going to budge, so it was time to pull out my big guns. I grabbed my phone and dialed the number of the one person who could help straighten this mess out.

Chapter 11

"WHO ARE YOU CALLING, Suzanne?" George asked me skeptically.

"You'll see," I said as Angelica answered. I put it on speaker so George could be a part of the conversation too.

"Hello? Suzanne? Are you there?"

George shook his head violently and made a throat-cutting motion for me to kill the call.

I never was very good at taking orders.

"I found out why George has been acting so strange lately," I said, and then I stuck my tongue out at him. It wasn't the most dignified thing I could do, but I had fun doing it. "He wants to quit his job, sell his house, and move to Union Square to be closer to you."

"What an idiot that man can be," she said, and I suddenly realized that I hadn't warned her that George was on the call too.

I quickly answered, "He's here with me. I thought you could quit dancing around the issues and talk to him directly." It was a gamble, and I knew it, but I cared too much for them both to worry about any toes I might be stepping on.

"George? Are you really there?" Angelica asked tentatively.

"I'm here. Do you really think I'm an idiot?" he asked her, though there was a hint of affection in his voice as he asked the question.

"I know you are if you quit your job for me," she said firmly.

George slumped down where he stood, and I felt bad about making this conversation happen after all. Had I just played a role in breaking the two of them up?

"You don't want to see more of me?" he asked, clearly crestfallen.

"Of course I do, but you *love* your job, and don't try to tell me otherwise."

"I love you more," he said haltingly.

There was a pause on the other end of the line before Angelica spoke again. "What did you just say?"

"Nothing," he answered, clearly regretting making the declaration in front of me or maybe even at all.

"You can't take it back now. You love me," Angelica said, her voice holding a touch of wonder in it as she said it.

"Blast it all, woman, of course I love you. What's not to love? You're amazing. It's just a shame you don't feel the same way about me," George told her, giving me a look of anger that I hadn't seen from him in quite some time.

"I never said that," Angelica answered.

"Your lack of a response spoke volumes," the mayor said. "Suzanne, hang up the phone."

"Suzanne Hart, if you disconnect this call, you will never be welcome at Napoli's again," Angelica said fiercely.

"You heard her," I told George. "I'm not about to take that chance. I'm sorry."

I truly was too. I had hoped to get them closer together, not drive them apart. Hurting two of my best friends was the worst outcome I could have imagined happening because of my interference.

"Then I'll just leave," George said. "Good bye, Angelica."

"I love you too, you big idiot," she said firmly, and I could hear a few gasps in the background.

Evidently George hadn't been the only one with an audience. Angelica's girls, at least some of them, had been there on her end, listening to her side of the conversation.

"If I'm such an idiot, why do you love me?" George asked, getting a bit of a stupid grin on his face as he said it.

"I must be an idiot too," she answered, clearly smiling. There were more gasps in the background, and I knew the girls were getting quite a show on their end as well. "But you mustn't quit your job or move here because of me. Do you understand that?"

"No," he said. "Don't you *want* me closer?"

"Of course I do, but things are going great between us, and I don't want to risk losing that. For now, let's just keep doing what we've been doing and see where it leads us."

"What about when my job keeps us apart?" he asked softly.

"We will deal with it," she said. "Suzanne came by last night and talked some sense into me, so I'll be better. I promise."

"I don't want you to feel as though you are *ever* my second choice," George said, actually blushing a bit as he said it.

"I won't anymore," she said. "Now get off Suzanne's phone, get in your truck, and come see me. I want to give you a kiss that you won't soon forget."

In the background I heard Sophia say, "Woooohoooo!"

"Hush, child," Angelica told her daughter, but there was nothing but love in the command. "Now, can you do that without quitting your job or selling your house?"

"I'll be there in ten minutes," George said.

"It's a thirty-minute drive," Angelica reminded him.

"Not today it's not," George answered as he bolted for the door. "Unlock this blasted thing so I can get out, Suzanne."

"You actually locked him in your shop to make him work this out with me?" Angelica asked me after George was out the door and on his way.

"Kind of," I admitted. "I'm sorry I butted in. I violated your privacy, but I just couldn't stand there and watch you two make the biggest mistakes of your lives."

"You're forgiven," she said and then added, "This time."

"Thanks. Let me know how it goes," I told her.

"I will not," she said with a laugh. "You are a twice-married woman. Use your imagination."

After she hung up, I went about cleaning the donut shop. I didn't even mind doing Emma's work as well as my own. If nothing else, at least some good had come from my meddling.

As I ran the report on my register and balanced out the drawer, I started thinking about what I could do to solve Richard Covington's murder. The man had virtually died in my arms, and besides that, Paige had asked me for my help, so there was no way I could just leave it to the police to figure out.

When he'd run to me, slapping his bloody hand on my window, he'd been asking for my help.

I hadn't been able to save him, but I was going to do my best to make sure that at least he hadn't died in vain.

Once everything was finished at the donut shop, I grabbed the leftover donuts for the day and thought that maybe I should have continued selling questions for a dozen treats instead of one. I had a good three dozen left, and now I had to find them a good home for them or end up throwing them out, something I couldn't bear to do.

After I had my Jeep loaded up with the extras, I swung by the bank to make my deposit before I took off for Maple Hollow. Too many trails led there, so I needed to head to the source. Who could I call to go with me, though? Grace was gone, Momma was tied up with her new assistant, George was busy working things out with Angelica, and Jake was out of town.

That left one person I had worked with before, though.

I just hoped he was free.

I knocked on his door and found him frowning at an old newspaper clipping in his hand. "Your mother isn't here, Suzanne," Phillip, my stepfather and the former police chief for April Springs, said.

"I wasn't looking for her. Do you have a second?"

"Sure," he said as he ran a hand through his hair. "I'm not making any progress on this thing, so I could use a distraction."

"Are you working on another cold case?" I asked him.

Phillip had made a hobby of researching long-buried cases after he'd retired from the force, and he'd actually had a bit of luck doing it. It kept him busy while Momma ran her empire, and in my opinion, it had made him a better cop than he'd been when he'd been our police chief, though I would never have dreamed of saying that to his face.

"It's a real puzzler," he admitted.

"Is it a murder?" I asked, knowing that I had to let him tell me about it before I could ask him what I'd come there to propose.

"There was a murder too, but mainly it's a theft," he answered.

I remembered our investigation earlier into locating the Southern Shooting Star, something that might someday be profitable for us all.

"It's another jewel, maybe even more spectacular than the last one," he conceded. "And we both know that those don't come along every day. A large diamond went missing over a hundred years ago, and some folks think it's still hidden somewhere in the western North Carolina hills."

"Does it have a cool name too?" I asked him as I tapped the faded newspaper clipping.

"No, it was just called the Egg," he told me.

"Not nearly as dramatic, is it?" I asked him.

"Maybe not, but it was an egg-shaped diamond pendant, so you can forgive them for not being very creative about naming it," he said. "Anyway, I figured if I could find enough clues, the four of us could take another vacation and go look for it."

I remembered the last time we'd done that and the bodies we'd left in our wake. "What are the odds of finding it?"

"Right now? Pretty terrible. I'm going to have to go check things out myself before I'm ready to go for it," he answered. "But not in the snow or even the cold. Maybe next summer." He nodded to himself, put the clipping on top of a pile on his desk, and then said, "You didn't come by to hear me ramble on about a wild goose chase. What's on your mind?" Then it suddenly occurred to him what had happened to me earlier. "I'm an idiot."

"Why do people keep saying that?" I asked him.

"Somebody else called me one too?" Phillip asked, clearly puzzled by my statement.

"No, other people talking about themselves, actually," I corrected.

"How are you doing? I heard about the murder in front of your shop this morning."

"I'm okay," I told him, which was true enough. "I need your help, though."

He nodded. "Name it. I'll do anything I can; you know that. Do you want to talk about what happened?" It was clear the offer made him uncomfortable, but it touched me that he was willing to make it nonetheless.

"Not talk, *do*," I said. "I want to see if I can dig up anything about the man who was murdered. He was originally from Maple Hollow, and we both know Momma would pitch a fit if I investigated on my own."

"I'm flattered," Phillip said, "but I *can't* be your first choice."

I could have lied to him, but I'd grown to respect the man too much to do that. "Momma's got her hands full with Geneva, Grace and Jake are out of town, and George is trying to straighten out his love life."

"So that makes me fifth on your list," he answered.

"Guilty as charged," I told him. It was not time to try to sugarcoat it.

"Hey, I'm just happy I made the cut," he said with a shrug. "Let me grab my jacket, and we can go."

After doing just that, he stopped and pulled out his phone. "I just need to send a quick text to your mother to tell her what we're up to."

"Tell her I said hello."

"Will do."

After he finished and put his cell phone away, I said, "Phillip, I'm happy you're free to help me. You know that, don't you?"

"I do. Maybe this is just what I need. I've been obsessing about that blasted egg long enough. It's time to get back to the present."

Once we were outside, he headed for his truck while I started for my Jeep.

"I thought I'd drive," I told him.

"I'd be happy to," he countered.

"Sure, but *I* have donuts," I replied with a smile.

"You should drive then," he answered in kind.

I let him sample the boxes in back, and then I got in, and we headed to Maple Hollow.

As we started off, Phillip asked, "What do you have so far?"

"Richard Covington was implicated in stealing a gold coin from Paige Hill when they both lived in Maple Hollow. He came back yesterday to try to make amends, but she shut him down. I was there, and it wasn't pretty. Evidently, he tried again later, and Paige rebuffed him yet again."

"How did he die?" Phillip asked, taking it all in.

"It was either an ice pick to the back of the neck or a blow to the head," I told him. "The new coroner, who also happens to be from Maple Hollow, couldn't be sure."

"Zoey Hicks. I've heard about her," my stepfather said.

"Really? I thought she was new."

"She is, but there was a rumor going around St. Dunbar that she had a huge crush on their married police chief, and things got ugly. The job opened up in Maple Hollow for a doctor, and she jumped all over it."

I risked a quick glance in his direction. "How could you possibly know that?"

"Do you remember a cop named Brewster who used to work for me?" he asked.

"Vaguely," I said. "That was before I started digging into things around here myself." That was putting it mildly, and I knew it. I'd been a thorn in the chief's side from the day Patrick Blaine had been murdered until the moment he'd retired from the force. I didn't regret it, either. After all, that had been the catalyst that had brought Jake into my life.

"Yeah, he left here to join the St. Dunbar force about the time you married Max," he explained. "Anyway, we keep in touch, and he texted me three months ago about what happened. The chief had to resign, and they named someone else as his replacement, even though Brewster thought he should have gotten the job. He moaned about the injustice of it all, and I heard more about Zoey Hicks than I ever wanted to hear."

"Do you think we should keep an eye on her?" I asked him.

"Why do you ask that?"

"When she came to confirm that Richard Covington was dead this morning, she was clearly flirting with Chief Grant." I hated even saying it out loud, but I felt the need to see what Phillip thought about the situation.

"No, he's fine," my stepfather said.

"How can you be so sure?" I asked.

"Well, for starters, the chief in St. Dunbar was messing around with more than one citizen there, if you get my drift, and for another, I've seen the way Stephen Grant looks at Grace. It's almost as intense as the way Jake looks at you."

"Does he really?" I asked. I'd noticed it, but I hadn't realized that anyone else could see it too.

"Come on, Suzanne, that man's as smitten with you as I am with your mother, and we both know how much that is," he answered with a smile.

"We do at that," I said. I hadn't been all that thrilled about the union at first, but I'd grown to realize that the former police chief loved my mother completely, sincerely, and intensely, and she returned it in kind. "Still, I'm going to say something to Grace when I get the chance."

"You wouldn't be you if you didn't," he answered with a smile, and then he polished off his second and last donut.

"What does that mean?" I asked him a bit sharply.

"Hey, I'm on your side, remember? All I'm saying is heaven help anyone who gets between you and your friends."

"Family too," I said as I patted his knee, suddenly sorry for my outburst.

"Family too," he echoed. "Right back at you, kiddo," he added.

"My dad used to call me that," I told him.

"Sorry. I didn't mean any harm in it," he apologized quickly.

"No, I like it. Just don't wear it out, okay?" I asked him with a slight smile.

He nodded. "Got it. Now, what else do you know about the man, or is that it?"

"No, I've got a little more," I said. "Evidently he and Geneva dated for a few months before she moved away from Maple Hollow when they were in high school. He didn't want a long-distance thing, but Paige said that Geneva took it badly. We were wondering if that was who we saw Geneva with at Napoli's last night."

"You ate at Napoli's?" he asked, the envy thick in his voice.

"*That's* your takeaway from what I just said?" I asked him with a grin.

"No, I heard you. A man died in front of you this morning, Suzanne. How could you not know if that was him you saw her with a few hours earlier?"

It was a fair question, even though I didn't care for the way it had sounded. "He was hidden from where I sat, but it was Geneva sure enough. I'm planning on asking her about it the next time I see her."

"Your mother isn't going to like that," Phillip said carefully.

"Tell me something I don't know, but what choice do I have? It could be important."

"I know that. Just tread lightly. That's all I'm saying," he answered.

"I will."

"Where should we go first when we get to town?" Phillip asked.

"I thought we might swing by the police chief's office," I admitted.

My stepfather looked stunned by my admission. "Seriously? I thought you tried to avoid the police when you were digging into murder."

"Usually I do, but from my past experience with Chief Holmes, that might be a bad idea. There's a chance I can get her blessing to dig a little, but if she catches us in town without talking to her first, there could be problems."

"You don't have to tell me that," Phillip said. "I remember how *I* felt when folks started nosing around in my cases." The last bit was spoken with the hint of a smile, and there was no doubt in my mind that it was meant for me.

"Point taken," I answered with a slight chuckle. "After that, I figured we could do a little digging around town. I know Richard was staying with an old friend named Rudy Francis, but I thought we might check out Burt's before we head there for any gossip about what's happening in town."

"I'm a longtime fan of the place myself," he said. "It sounds like a solid approach to me. I only have one question."

"Just one?" I asked him.

"What if the chief says no?"

"Well, she can't keep us from eating, can she? I've got a feeling that Richard Covington is all that folks at Burt's will be talking about. If we listen really hard, we might just get a clue about what to do next."

"Even if we don't get the chief's approval?" Phillip asked me sincerely.

"Even then," I told him firmly. "Is that going to be a problem for you?"

"No, ma'am. No problem at all. Just asking."

We drove into the city limits of Maple Hollow where the antiques stores all were, and I thought about my Aunt Jean, who had been murdered in this town not all that long ago. It still held bad memories for me, but I had a job to do, an obligation, and I wasn't about to let the ghosts from my past keep me from working in the present.

Next, we drove past the old high school, closed now and set for demolition soon, according to gossip I'd picked up at the donut shop. The team mascot had clearly been a bulldog, because there was an old statue of one in front of the main building sitting atop a crumbling old brick pedestal, a testament to times past, and no doubt slated for removal soon as well.

I started for the police station when I noticed a police cruiser parked in front of Marcast, a gallery owned by Martin Lancaster, a man who wasn't exactly my biggest fan because of our earlier run-ins.

I couldn't wait for the chief to leave there, though. I needed to get the ball rolling on our investigation into Richard Covington's murder.

I parked beside the squad car and got out just as Chief Holmes came out of the shop, nudging a handcuffed man in front of her toward her vehicle.

Chapter 12

"IT'S BEEN AWHILE," Chief Holmes said as she approached us with her suspect. "No offense, but I was kind of hoping you'd forgotten all about us here in Maple Hollow, Suzanne. Who is this with you this afternoon?"

"I'm the former police chief for April Springs. The name's Phillip Martin, Chief."

She nodded. "I'd shake your hand, but I'm kind of busy at the moment."

"I didn't steal anything! You don't have any right to arrest me, you crazy pig woman!" the man she had cuffed shouted at her.

"Mr. Jenkins, I told you before that you needed to be civil, and I won't tell you again," she said in a calm voice, dismissing him for a moment with one cold stare.

He was clearly unhappy about the warning, but he didn't say anything else, so perhaps he'd gotten her message after all. Chief Liddy Holmes was not a woman to mess with, and he wasn't doing himself any favors by antagonizing her.

"We just wanted to let you know that we were in town," I said.

"This is about Richard Covington," she answered, figuring it out instantly. "He died right in front of you last night, didn't he?"

"Yes, ma'am, but actually it was early this morning," I said with all due respect. Had it really been that recent? Time had a way of flying past sometimes. "We won't get in your way, but we're going to nose around a bit, with your permission."

"The murder happened outside of my jurisdiction, but do you honestly think you can come here with a former police chief and dig into something that is frankly none of your business?" she asked.

"He's not just the former chief; he's my stepfather too. We're not going to do *anything* but ask a few questions," I said as I nodded toward Phillip.

She was about to reply when the man she had cuffed decided to make a break for it. Where he thought he was going I could not say, but almost instinctively, I stuck out my foot and tripped him. Jenkins tumbled onto the grass beside the sidewalk, landing fairly safely, but he hadn't been able to brace himself for the fall since he'd been cuffed with his hands behind his back, and there was a bit of blood coming from his nose, though it appeared that he'd avoided any real damage.

"Mr. Jenkins, are you okay? That was a nasty fall you just took. You need to be more careful when you're walking," the chief said as she yanked him back up to his feet.

"That stupid cow knocked me down!" he screamed as he made a move toward me.

"I don't know what you're talking about," the chief said calmly as she easily pulled him back. "All *I* saw was that you tried to get away from being in custody, you tripped on the sidewalk, and then you fell onto the grass."

"She broke my nose!" the man yelled at me.

Chief Holmes didn't have any patience left for the man. "I'm sure you'll be fine, but we'll get someone to take a look at that for you. Come on, let's get you to the station."

The chief of police got him in the back of the car—under his protests—and after she slammed the door shut, she came back and joined us.

"If you need to go, we understand," I told her. "He's quite a handful, isn't he?"

Without looking back at him, the chief said softly, "It's turning out that way. Lancaster doesn't want him prosecuted. He just wanted me to escort him from the building."

"Then why is he in cuffs?" Phillip asked her.

"He took a swing at me," she said.

"And he lived to tell about it?" I asked her.

The expression she gave me was one that chilled me to the core. "I'm not some kind of animal, Mrs. Bishop; I'm a law enforcement professional. Oh, that's right, you still go by Hart, don't you?"

"I didn't mean it that way at all," I explained quickly. "As a matter of fact, I think you showed remarkable restraint. I'm confused, though. Why would Martin Lancaster *not* want someone prosecuted for stealing from him? I've had a few run-ins with him in the past, and he didn't exactly strike me as the forgiving type."

The law officer shrugged. "Evidently he's the man's third cousin or something like that. Anyway, I'm trying to decide what to do with him now. I was going to let him cool off a bit in a cell and then turn him loose, but that spill he took has got him so riled up that I'm not sure what I'm going to do. Sometimes I hate small-town politics," she added almost as an afterthought.

"It's part of the job though, isn't it?" Phillip asked.

"You were smart to get out," she said in commiseration.

"It was time for me, but you're still young," Phillip replied.

"Relatively speaking," she replied. "Listen, I can't keep you from asking a few questions, but don't push me, okay? I get why you're vested in this, but I can only look the other way so long. Chief Grant has asked me to look into a few things, and I can guarantee you that it won't be long until the state police get involved, so you need to tread lightly. Do you both read me?"

"Loud and clear," we said in near unison.

She smiled for the first time since we'd seen her that day. "You two should take that act on the road. Anyplace but Maple Hollow, maybe," she added, the smile vanishing.

"Thank you, Chief," I said.

"You're welcome. Tell your husband to come by the station sometime. I'd like a chance to catch up on how retired life has been treating him."

She wasn't a threat, not because she wasn't attractive but because I knew that my husband only had eyes for me. "I will, but don't expect it any time soon. He's working on a case in western North Carolina at the moment, a puzzling murder."

"Some people have all of the luck," she said offhandedly, and then she got into her car and drove off without another look back at us.

"She's one cool customer," Phillip said admiringly.

"*I'd* hate to cross her," I replied.

"Then let's not, okay? We do a little digging, ask a few questions, and see where it gets us, but we do our best not to cross the line."

"I'm good with that," I said as we got back into the Jeep. "Only how do we know where the line is?"

"When we cross it, we'll both know," he answered. "In the meantime, let's head over to Burt's. I'm hungry."

"We're here to ask questions, not have lunch," I reminded him.

"Is there any law that says we can't do both?" he asked me with a grin.

"None that I know of," I agreed.

"Well then, there you go."

Burt's hadn't changed a bit since I'd been there last with my husband. It sported the same worn linoleum floor, scratched Formica tabletops, and faded yellow walls. We grabbed an open booth, and an old friend from before approached us.

"Why as I live and breathe, it's Suzanne Hart," Tammy said. "I thought we'd seen the last of you, girl." Tammy still wore the same granny glasses, and her blonde hair was starting to go a bit gray, but it was clear that age hadn't dulled her snappy spirit.

"It's good to see you, Tammy," I said. "This is my stepfather, Phillip."

"Hello there, Phillip. I had to figure you were already married, a good-looking man like you," she said with a laugh.

"She's just saying it for the tip," I told him, winking at the waitress.

"Sometimes that's true enough, but this time I mean every last word of it."

Phillip had the grace to blush a bit. "I don't...er...know what to say."

"That's the point, sugar," she told him. "Sweet tea?"

"Times two," I said. "Is Penny still making it too sweet?"

"Whenever I turn my back, she does," Tammy said. "Burt's whipped up something special in the kitchen today."

"We'll take two of them," I said, remembering how amazing the man's food had been, and then I turned to Phillip. "Is that okay with you? Trust me, you can't go wrong betting on this man's food."

"I've eaten here before, remember? I'm game if you are," he said.

"That's what I like, folks willing to roll the dice," Tammy said.

A few moments later, she returned with a pair of sweet teas. I took a sip of mine. "Wow, that's even sweeter than the last time I was here."

"She's getting worse and worse," Tammy said, "but try telling her that."

After our server was gone, I looked around and saw that folks started talking among themselves again. When we'd first come in, things had gotten kind of quiet, us being strangers and all, but after hearing us banter with Tammy, they must have believed that we were okay.

One older man turned to his friend, ignoring us, which was exactly what I'd hoped they'd do. "They found him with the rock still stuck in the back of his head," the man said, shaking his head in wonder.

Phillip started to correct the misinformation, but I put a hand on him and shook my head slightly. He nodded and then shrugged an apology in my direction.

After all, we were there to learn, not to teach.

"They found him in front of a pie shop, I heard," his companion said.

It was all I could do to keep my mouth shut that time, but somehow I managed it. Finally, someone near them added, "It was donuts. I've had them before. They're mighty tasty."

"Freddy, we've *all* had donuts before. We know they're good," the first man said with clear disdain.

"I'm talking about this place in particular. It's called Donut Holes or something like that."

Again, I had to keep my mouth shut. I looked over at my stepfather, who was clearly enjoying my discomfort. He just smiled broadly at me, though I couldn't return it.

"Hurts, I think it is," his companion said.

"Donut Hurts? Really? What kind of stupid name is that?" another man asked.

"Hey, it's April Springs. That's not the *dumbest* name they have in town. There's a bookstore there called the Chapter 11, if that don't beat all."

"It's the Last Chapter," someone else said.

It was The Last Page, but again, I didn't correct anybody, though it took about every ounce of energy I had.

"It's still a crazy name if you ask me. How's Rudy taking it? When those boys were growing up, Mrs. Francis always used to say that she had *two* sons, one natural and one adopted. I heard Richie was staying with him at the house."

"He likes to be called Richard now," a nearby woman corrected him.

"The truth is, he doesn't care *what* we call him since last night," the original man said.

"You've got a point. Boy oh boy, that's a tough way to go. I wonder what Christy Smucker thinks about him coming back home just to get himself killed."

"They were old news," the woman who'd interjected earlier said.

"That's what you think," the man added with a wink. "Roy Buck-walter saw Christy slipping out of Rudy's place the night before last at three o'clock in the morning, and you can bet your bottom dollar she wasn't there to see Rudy, no matter how much he wished otherwise. That man's had a crush on her since they were all in the third grade together, but she's never had eyes for anybody but Richie, I mean Richard."

"You are kidding me," the woman said, her voice clearly filled with wonder. "They were taking back up together? Seriously?"

"I wouldn't pull your leg, Gladys," he said.

"Hiram, if you ever tried, you'd be pulling back a stub, and we both know it."

"Come on, Gladdy, you know you love me," Hiram said with a smile that was missing a few teeth.

"In your dreams, old man," Gladys said, though if I had to guess, I would have said that they were about the same age or close enough not to matter.

"Every night, sugar, and you know it," he said.

"Don't make me come over there and smack you, you old fool," she cautioned, though I noticed that she was doing everything in her power to suppress the smile she was fighting.

"Don't make promises you aren't willing to keep, girl," Hiram said, and then he laughed. It took Gladys a second to join in, but soon the entire gossip squad was smiling over it.

Before they could start up again, Tammy came by with our plates. "Here you go. Eat up, folks," she said as she slid the bill under Phillip's plate.

"What makes you think she's not treating me to lunch?" he asked her with a smile.

"You look like too much of a gentleman to let a lady buy your meal," she answered.

"That's true enough," Phillip said as he looked at the plate. "Is this Salisbury steak? I was hoping for something a little more exotic." There was a hint of disappointment in his voice as he said it, but Tammy didn't take offense.

"Taste the gravy," she told him matter-of-factly.

Phillip did as instructed, and after that spoon left his lips, he broke out into a big grin. "I sit corrected," he said. "That's amazing."

"Burt always aims to please," Tammy answered.

"If everything else is this good, he's succeeded beyond my wildest expectation."

"Enjoy now, you hear?" she asked as she turned to another table. "Refills on those teas, folks?"

"Thank you kindly, but we've got to get going," Hiram said.

"Where are you off to this afternoon?" Tammy asked him.

"We're doing a little birdwatching at the old pond," he said.

"What kind of birds are you hoping to spot?" she asked him.

"Well, I'd love to see Gladdy over there in my binoculars, but if not, I'll just have to settle for something a tad less exotic."

"Hiram Wilmoth, one of these days, I'm going to call your bluff. You know that, don't you?"

"You keep threatening to do it, but I'm still holding my breath and counting the days," he answered as they both stood.

To everyone in the diner's surprise and delight, including, it appeared, Gladys, she reached over, grabbed his head in her hands, and then laid a powerful kiss on him that no doubt curled his toes.

As she broke free, the entire diner, including Phillip and I, started clapping and whistling.

Gladys took a bow, and then she turned back to the blushing and clearly stunned Hiram. "What do you think about that, sport?"

"I'm not sure yet," he admitted, clearly a bit dazed by the attention. "As soon as my eyes roll back into my head, I'll let you know. Wow, just wow. That's all I can say at the moment."

"I think that says enough," Gladys said, giving her rump a little shake on the way out the door.

"Gladys, I hate to spoil your exit, but you forgot to pay," Tammy reminded her.

"You'll take care of it, won't you, Hiram?" she asked him.

"Any time, any place," Hiram said.

"That's what I thought," she responded with a bit of a giggle as she sashayed out of Burt's.

The food was sublime, but it was all that I could do to make myself slow down enough to taste it. We had not one but two people to interview now, Rudy Francis and Christy Smucker. It sounded as though Rudy was jealous of his old friend, but how much of a torch did he still carry for a girl from his school days? I knew how powerful young love could be, so it wasn't completely out of the realm of possibility, especially if the two of them had rubbed his nose in it. As for Christy, what if she and Richard had argued over something after trying to work things out again, namely Paige or even Geneva? I knew that love triangles could spell disaster for everyone involved, and I imagined that a love square would be even worse. How had Richard gotten *three* women interested in him? I'd met the man, and while he'd been handsome enough, he hadn't struck me as being anything great in the personality department.

Then again, maybe that wasn't as important to some people as it was to me.

We would see soon enough, that was for sure.

Chapter 13

"SO, WHO DO WE TACKLE first, Christy or Rudy?" Phillip asked as we started to walk back to my Jeep. "You do want to talk to them both, don't you?"

"I do," I admitted as we got in. "I was thinking we'd speak with Christy first."

"Really?" Phillip asked me.

"Yes, really. I'm guessing you'd like to talk to Rudy," I said.

"No, your way is fine. I'm just wondering why, though."

"It's simple enough," I admitted. "There's no doubt in my mind that Chief Holmes has already been to Rudy's, but there's a slim chance she hasn't found out about Christy and Richard going out again recently, so we might catch her off guard if we speak with her first."

"That's good, solid investigative reasoning," Phillip said.

"Are you making fun of me?" I asked him as I glanced over in his direction.

"No, ma'am, quite the contrary. I see your point, and I agree with you."

"Wow, you really *do* take me seriously these days, don't you?" I asked him. "It's a far cry from how you acted when you were still the police chief."

"Hey, old dogs *can* learn new tricks, despite the saying," he answered. "I admit I was wrong before."

"Thanks. It's good to hear," I told him as I pulled out my cell phone.

"Who are you calling?" Phillip asked me. "You're not giving her a warning that we're coming, are you?"

"No, but we need to find out where they both live," I said. "I figured I'd just Google it."

"We can do better than that," he said as he pointed to someone leaving Burt's.

It was Tammy, and from the looks of it, she was heading off somewhere, and in quite a hurry to get there too.

"I wonder where she's going," I mused as we watched her hustle down the street.

"I'm guessing it's to warn either Christy or Rudy," Phillip answered.

"Why would she do that? I thought we were on a friendly basis with her," I said as I started the Jeep and crept down the street behind her, trying to keep her in sight but not warn her as to what we were up to.

"We are, but they're from Maple Hollow, and we're not," my stepfather said. "Put yourself in her shoes. Wouldn't you look out for our folks before you helped someone from out of town?"

"I suppose I would," I answered. "She could be going home for lunch, you know."

"Let me ask you something. If you worked at Burt's, would you eat anywhere else?" Phillip asked.

"No, I don't suppose I would." I pulled over again to give her more time to get ahead of us. "Should we continue this on foot?"

"We could, but we'll stick out even more if we do. Let's give her a minute."

"In the meantime, I'll get us those addresses," I said as I pulled out my phone again. "Okay, Christy is on Dunbar Avenue, and Rudy is on St. Albans Drive."

"Can you tell which direction she's heading?" Phillip asked me.

"Hang on." I called up my Maps app and saw that St. Albans was in the opposite direction, but Dunbar was close. "She's headed to Christy's place," I added as I started up the Jeep and took off again.

"Slow down. She's going to see us," Phillip cautioned me.

"She already knows where we're going," I told him. "Wave," I instructed as we passed her, and I tooted my horn briefly.

Tammy didn't look all that pleased to see us overtaking her, but she put on a brave face and waved back.

I decided to push my luck. I brought the Jeep to a halt and rolled down Phillip's window. "Can we give you a lift someplace?"

She grinned at me. "I have a feeling we're heading in the same direction. Christy didn't answer her phone when I called her to give her a heads-up that you might be on your way, so I wanted to touch base with her before you got around to looking her up."

"I can appreciate that, but we're not trying to stir up trouble," I told her.

"Maybe yes, maybe no, but she's my friend, and I need to look out for her."

I had a sudden thought. "Why don't you go with us, if you feel that way? If we get too carried away, you can always rein us in."

Tammy shook her head. "I appreciate the offer, but I trust you to do the right thing." The waitress turned and headed back up the street without another glance back at us.

"What was that all about?" Phillip asked me as I started driving again.

"You heard the woman. She trusts us, at least at the moment."

"Should she, though?" he asked me.

"We need to ask Christy about Richard Covington, but we have to be delicate about it," I admitted. "We can do that, right?"

"Suzanne, I haven't used my 'cop voice' in a long time, and you know it," my stepfather said with a shrug. "You taught me that."

"Just checking," I told him with a smile. "Are you ready for this?" I added as we pulled into the driveway of a bungalow barely big enough for one. It was well kept, but I would have hated to try to fit more than one person inside it.

"I'm ready."

"You're Christy Smucker, right?" I asked when she answered the door. She was a woman about my age, but the years hadn't been as kind to her as they had to me. From the lines on her face and her hang-dog expression, I had a feeling that she'd had more than her share of rough times.

"I am," she admitted. "You must be Tammy's friends."

That caught me by surprise. "She finally got ahold of you?" I asked.

"I had my ringer off. I was trying to take a nap, but I finally figured out it was useless. When I turned it back on, I had two messages from Tammy."

"The first one was warning you that we were on our way," I said without having to guess. "Did the second one mention that you could trust us?"

She looked at me with a hint of wonder. "Are you some kind of mind reader or something?"

"No, ma'am. I make donuts for a living. I'm Suzanne Hart, and this is my stepfather, Phillip Martin."

She didn't take our offered hands, but she did nod at each of us. "Were you friends of Richard's?" she asked gently.

Maybe I should have lied, but I just couldn't bring myself to do it. "We met yesterday for the first time," I admitted, "and I didn't spend more than three minutes talking to him. Phillip never met him at all."

Christy frowned. "Then why are you here in town, asking questions about him?"

"He practically died in my arms," I told her, not trying to shade the truth in any way. "I feel a responsibility toward him because of it, and I've had a little luck in the past figuring these things out. I decided that I at least owed him that much." We were still standing outside her place, but she didn't invite us in. I honestly wasn't sure there was even room for all three of us inside if she'd asked.

"He had breakfast here the day before yesterday, and that was the last time I saw him, did you know that? I can't believe he's gone."

"What did you two talk about?" Phillip asked gently.

"This and that," Christy replied, clearly unhappy about his question.

"Did the two of you argue by any chance?" I probed softly.

The woman again looked at me as though I'd grown a third eye. "Now you're officially spooking me out. How did you know?"

"You seem troubled," I told her. "Maybe it would help to get it all out into the open. I know I always feel better when I tell someone my troubles."

Phillip started to say something, but with a brief shake of my head, I stopped him. Now it was time to let Christy decide if she was going to speak with us or not.

"Maybe you're right," she said after a pregnant pause. "I told him that I wanted to be with him, and I thought he felt the same way about me, but there were some things he had to take care of first. At least that's what he said." Her cheeks blushed a bit as she added, "I'm afraid I didn't take it well. I accused him of using me, but he swore he wanted to be with me. I lashed out at him, and I regretted it the second I watched him drive that truck of his away, but by then, it was too late. I tried to call him to apologize, but he never picked up."

"Did you at least leave him a voicemail?" I asked her.

"Yes. I explained it all to him, how I had been unfair to judge him on the behavior of a few bad seeds that had come before him. I wish I could know if he heard it or not."

"I'm certain that he did," I said.

"How can you be so sure?"

"Richard didn't strike me as the type of person to let a voicemail go unheard," I told her.

Whether he really was or not, I couldn't say, but I had to give her at least a sliver of hope that he had. After all, she was going to have to live with what had happened for a very long time. It was something that I wouldn't have wished on anyone, and it was also one of the reasons I always wanted Jake to know that I loved him every time we hung up. In his line of work—shoot, even in my avocation of investigating murder—I could never be sure when I said goodbye that I'd ever have the chance to speak to him again.

"I so hope you are right," she said.

"Christy, do you have *any* idea what loose ends he was trying to wrap up?" Phillip asked her.

It was a good question, and what was more, he'd posed it in such a way that made him seem caring and not just probing for answers.

"I have a few hunches," she admitted. "There's a woman in April Springs named Paige Hill he was desperate to talk to, but I don't think it was romantic."

"It wasn't," I assured her. "Paige is a friend of mine. She told me all about their conversation last night."

Christy's expression darkened. "She seemed important to him."

"For other reasons," I explained. "Anything else?"

"Geneva Swift was trying to get her hooks in him again," Christy said with disdain. "That woman is absolutely shameless. Richard told her that he wasn't interested in her, but she kept after him."

"When did he tell you that?" I asked.

"Yester...the day before yesterday, I mean," Christy said.

Was that an honest mistake, or was she lying to us now? She said she hadn't spoken with the murder victim since breakfast the day before yesterday, but now I was beginning to wonder.

There was no point pushing her on it at the moment, though.

"Is that it?" Phillip asked her.

"Yes," she said after too long a pause.

That was clearly another lie, and one I couldn't just let go. "Christy, we can't help find Richard's killer and help avenge his death if you aren't honest with us," I said gravely.

Maybe I was laying it on a little thick, but it was true nonetheless.

After ten long seconds of nothing but silence, she finally relented. "Rudy."

"What about him?" I asked, already knowing that Christy had been a point of contention between the men.

"We went out a few times lately, but there wasn't any great spark there for me, you know? When Richard came back into town, it all came flooding back, and I knew that what I was feeling for Rudy was more friendship than anything else."

"Did you tell him that?" Phillip asked her softly.

"I had to. I couldn't keep leading him on," she said, and then she frowned a moment. "You don't think? No, it couldn't be."

"It might," I said. "When did you break things off with Rudy?" I followed up.

"Three nights ago," she admitted, and then she turned a little green around the gills. "Excuse me, I've got to go."

Before we could stop her, she bolted inside and latched the door firmly behind her.

"She's wrestling with the idea that Rudy did something to Richard because of her, isn't she?" I asked Phillip as we walked back to the Jeep.

"It's a troubling thought to have to consider," he said. "Do you think Rudy took the breakup hard enough to get rid of his competition?"

"I have to believe that it's at least possible," I replied. "Even if it's not, we need to go speak with Rudy."

"Should we touch base with Chief Holmes and tell her about Christy? It might get us a few brownie points with her, and I doubt Christy's going to tell us much else."

"Let's call her on the way to Rudy's," I said.

Phillip was right. What would it hurt to have a little goodwill with local law enforcement? Maybe, just maybe, the chief would give us a little more slack on the rope she was holding.

Then again, she might use it to make a noose to hang us with, but I chose to accentuate the positive.

Chapter 14

"CHIEF, DO YOU HAVE a second?" I asked as she picked up on the second ring.

"Are you on the road? You'd better be calling me on a hands-free device, Suzanne," she told me.

"Well, my stepfather is holding the phone, and I'm the one who's driving, so does that count as hands-free?" I asked her.

"It's fine. What can I do for you?"

"Did you know that Christy Smucker was seeing Richard Covington?" I asked her.

"Sure, back in school," she said.

"How did you know that? You aren't from around here," I said.

"No, but I listen when folks talk. What about it?"

"They were starting up again where they left off," I said. "The two of them had breakfast together the day before yesterday, and what's more, they argued." I decided to keep my guesses to myself and stick to just what I knew for a fact or at least what I'd been told.

"And how exactly do you know that?"

"We had lunch at Burt's," Phillip interjected. "You know how much you can overhear when you're not meaning to."

"You can hear even more when that's your intent," she said, clearly a little miffed that we'd scooped her on something. "I take it you're just leaving Ms. Smucker's house?"

"I can't deny it," I told her.

"Good. Wave to me as I drive past you," she said.

I looked up and saw her driving in the other direction, toward Christy Smucker's place and away from us.

I did as she instructed and waved to her.

All I got was a nod back.

"So, you knew all about her?" I asked her.

"Not until you just told me," she admitted. "Is there anything else I need to know?"

"Nothing we can think of," Phillip said before I could answer, "but we'll keep you posted."

"Be sure you do that," she said, and then, before I could add anything to the conversation, she ended the call.

"I'm not sure she wasn't holding her phone in her hands as she drove," I said.

"It's not illegal, at least not yet. It's just discouraged," Phillip answered.

"Was it my imagination, or did she seem a little terse with us just then?"

He shrugged. "We're stepping into an official investigation. Who can blame her?"

"Then why didn't she put up more of a fuss when we told her what we were up to?"

"My guess is that she respects what's she heard about you, but she respects Jake's reputation even more," Phillip answered.

"Then again, maybe she heard what a bang-up job you did when you were the police chief in April Springs."

"Maybe," he answered, but it was clear he didn't believe it. "Well, at least she didn't warn us away from going to see Rudy."

"She did not," I answered as we started getting closer to his home, at least according to the GPS on my phone. "Do you think maybe she's *using* us to shake her suspects up a little?"

"I wouldn't blame her if she did," Phillip said. "Nobody likes it when one of their citizens is killed and they're the one in charge."

"Even if it didn't happen here in town?" I asked.

"Even then," he answered.

"Well, let's see what we can do to get Rudy to talk. I want to know about his true relationship with Richard Covington, his feelings toward Christy Smucker, and anything he knows about Geneva Swift."

"Then we'd better get busy," Phillip said as the phone announced that we'd arrived at our destination.

The house was old, probably built in the sixties or seventies, and that might have been the last time the exterior had gotten a coat of fresh paint. Though it was getting colder out now, the yard had probably last been tended to in the warmth of summer. One of the front wooden steps was cracked and about to fall away from the nails holding it in place, so I skipped that one and did kind of a stretch to get up onto the front porch.

We rang the bell, waited a minute, and then rang it again.

I looked at Phillip. "Did you hear anything inside?"

"No, ma'am," he answered. "Suzanne, you're not going to try to break in and claim that you heard someone in there crying for help, are you?"

"Would I do that?" I asked as innocently as I could muster.

"Do you honestly want me to answer that?"

"Maybe not," I said as I pounded on the front door, skipping the doorbell entirely this time.

I heard some shuffling around inside, and then the front door opened. A man about my age, thin as a rail and sporting a mess of brown hair that was long overdue to be cut, answered. The shirttail on his left side was pulled out, though the right was still tucked in, and there was a bottle of whiskey in his hand as he waved us on.

"Thought I heard somebody out here. Come on in. The merrier the more, I mean, the more the merrier. Want a drink?"

"No, thank you," I said as I stepped in with Phillip on my heels.

"Come on. This is a wake for my good old buddy, Richie," he said, frowning. "Everybody knows you gotta drink at a wake."

"Maybe a small one," Phillip said.

Rudy winked at him. "You'll barely know it's even there," he said as he went into the kitchen for glasses.

"You're honestly going to drink with him?" I hissed.

"Of course not. Think of it more as protective camouflage," he whispered back. "We need to keep him talking, and if he thinks we're drinking with him, he'll be less likely to stonewall us, or worse, throw us out."

"That's good," I said softly, happy that Phillip had thought of it.

Rudy came back in with two mismatched glasses, held by two fingers of one hand, with each finger dipping well into the drinks he was trying to serve us.

At least it was alcohol. Maybe that would kill the germs on his hand, not that I was planning on drinking, anyway.

"How did you two know old Richie?" he asked us as he took a healthy swig of his own refilled glass of booze.

"We just met yesterday," I admitted, wanting to stay with the truth as long as I could.

"Yeah, well, he's going to be missed around here. By some more than others maybe, but I know that *I'll* sure miss him," he added as he took another large swallow. We were going to have to get to our questions quickly, because at the rate he was drinking, I doubted that he'd be alert, or even conscious, very much longer.

"We heard he was staying here with you," Phillip nudged him.

I had decided to let my stepfather handle most of the questions with Rudy. After all, he'd clearly had a great deal more experience dealing with drunken men than I had, something I was extremely thankful for.

"Yep," Rudy said as he took another swig. "Not that you'd know it. Right down there," he said as he pointed with his glass. "That crazy police chief came in and took everything Richie had. She nearly tore that room apart."

So I'd been right in believing that Chief Holmes had already been there. Most likely, she hadn't left anything behind, but it wasn't anything that I hadn't been expecting.

"I'm really sorry for your loss," I told him.

He looked up in surprise when I spoke, as though he'd forgotten that I was even there. "Yeah. It was tough losing him. He told me he came back here to make something right, to settle a few old scores, and to see a few old friends. I was touched, I tell you. Richie was going to leave Maple Hollow behind and never come back once he wrapped everything up, but it looks like he pushed one of them too hard, and they decided to push back."

"How is Christy taking it?" Phillip asked as he stared at the bottom of his glass. For all the world, he looked as though he could be as drunk as Rudy was, but I knew better.

This man was good, maybe even better than I gave him credit for.

"She's torn up, but she'll come back around, just you wait and see," Rudy said as he pointed his glass at Phillip this time. It was only then that he seemed to notice that his glass was empty. "Gotta get me some more. You two want some?" He eyed my glass. "You're not drinking." It was more of an accusation than a declarative statement.

I held the glass to my lips and took in a large amount, something that satisfied Rudy. "That's better. Be right back," he said as he clinked empty glasses with my stepfather.

The second he was out of the room, I emptied the liquor from my mouth back into my glass.

"Pour it in here," Phillip whispered as he pointed to a nearby potted plant that was clearly artificial.

"Won't he notice that?" I asked as I did it anyway.

"Sure, but it won't be until after he passes out, and we'll be long gone by then. That's where all of mine is," he added with a grin.

I left a splash in mine for authenticity, and Rudy looked at my glass approvingly as he came back in with a fresh bottle. "That's the spirit," he said happily, forgetting for a moment why we were there. After our glasses were topped off, he raised his. "To Richie."

"To Richie," we echoed, taking sips that ended back in our glasses again.

Rudy didn't notice, which didn't surprise me.

"So, Christy, huh?" Phillip asked. Was there really a question in there? It sounded like something a drunk would think of as a cogent thought.

"Yeah, she might not be a looker, but she can cook! Man, I miss home cooking, and that house of hers is as neat as a pin," he said wistfully.

Was he looking for a girlfriend or a servant? I had to bite my tongue from saying anything. After all, we weren't there to teach the man manners, though it was clear that someone should.

"But she took up with Richie again as soon as he came back to town, didn't she?" Phillip asked him.

"Yeah, well, my old friend had a way with the ladies, not that I could blame him for that. It was nothing, though. They never would have lasted." He pointed his glass again. "I told him there were greener pastures out there waiting for him in the big ol' world, and he was starting to come around to that way of thinking. The truth is that at one point, old Richie was even thinking about taking up with Geneva again. It was clear that she had the hots for him," he said as he stared into his glass. "Then, all of a sudden, out of nowhere, he changed his mind and told me he was done with both of them, Christy and Geneva included, and he wanted to forget that he'd ever known either one of them. You should have heard Geneva screaming last night when he told her he wasn't interested in her and never would be. Man, she started throwing crap—my crap, I might add—and we both had to duck and cover! Who knew that woman had such a bad temper? Ol' Richie was better off without her, without both of them." He stared a bit more, and I thought he was finished, but then he added, "I don't think he got around to telling Christy, though. That's why she's taking it so hard."

That wasn't the way we'd heard it, and it was pretty clear that *someone* was lying to us, but who? I decided to have a look around while I could. I knew that the chief and her people would be thorough, but what could it hurt to double-check? I stood suddenly and pretended to be sick. "I'm not doing so good all of a sudden. Where's your bathroom?"

"Down next to Richie's room," Rudy said with a laugh. "Can't hold your liquor, huh?" He almost sounded pleased by the idea.

"Excuse me," I said as I hurried down the hall.

I skipped the bathroom, though, and headed into the room that Richard Covington had occupied so recently so I could take a look around myself.

The guestroom was about what I expected after seeing the rest of Rudy's place. The sheets didn't match the pillowcases, and they were all worn to the point of being threadbare. The blanket had a few rips in it, and the nightstand had duct tape on one leg, barely managing to hold it in place. I checked the drawers of the cheap dresser, the one in the nightstand, and the closet shelf, but everything was empty. There was nothing there that gave any clue that anyone had stayed there within the past several days.

Chief Holmes had been thorough indeed.

I heard a disturbance out front and wondered what Rudy and Phillip were talking about. Their voices were getting louder, and I realized that I should get out of there before Rudy wondered what I was up to. Then I remembered that I had been supposed to be going to the bathroom. Would he realize that he hadn't heard a sink running or a toilet flushing, as drunk as he was? Probably not, but why take the chance? I ducked into the hallway and then into the bathroom, closing the door behind me. After giving the toilet a quick flush, I started washing my hands, and then I looked around for a towel.

There was one on the rack by the sink, but it didn't look all that hygienic to me, so I opened the small linen closet and looked for one there.

He had an odd collection of castoffs that Goodwill would turn their noses up at, but I dug the one out of the bottom of the stack, hoping for the best.

An envelope fell out of it.

I had just reached to pick it up when I heard a noise just outside the bathroom door!

"Hurry it up! Gotta get in there," Rudy shouted as he pounded hard, shaking the door in its frame.

I thought about putting the envelope back, but there was a weight to it that told me I should keep it. After jamming it into my pocket, I put the towel back where it had been when the doorknob rattled again. "Come on, lady. This is an emergency."

Evidently Rudy had finally overserved himself.

I threw the door open and got out of there as he brushed past me and slammed it behind him.

"Are you okay?" I asked him through the closed door.

"Just go, okay?" he pled, and then I heard him get sick.

Phillip touched my shoulder. "Let's go, Suzanne," he said softly.

"I'm right behind you."

Chapter 15

WE NEVER MADE IT TO the Jeep, though.

Somebody was lying in wait for us, and the moment we stepped off that porch, he attacked.

Chapter 16

PHILLIP SIDESTEPPED the charging man we'd seen Chief Holmes arrest earlier, and as he moved past my stepfather, I gave Jenkins a push in the back, sending him straight into a porch column. He hit his shoulder pretty hard, though I wouldn't have minded him hitting his head at that point.

As our attacker spun to recover his balance, he fell to the ground despite his best efforts. Jenkins had worked his way back to his hands and knees—clearly ready to come at us again—when he looked up to see Phillip's revolver staring him down.

"I didn't even know you had that with you," I told my stepfather breathlessly.

"Yeah, well, hanging out with you can be dangerous, so I thought I might need it," Phillip said.

"You think you're a big man with that big gun, don't you? Put that thing away and fight me like a real man, you coward," Jenkins said with a scowl.

Phillip laughed at him. "Now why would I want to do that? Suzanne, call Chief Holmes." Jenkins started to get up, but my stepfather said coolly, "I wouldn't advise that, if I were you."

"You're not going to shoot me," Jenkins said mockingly.

Phillip used the gun barrel and shoved the man backward. "Try me."

Clearly he still had his "cop" voice, because Jenkins suddenly reconsidered pushing his luck.

I called 9-1-1 and got the chief, who was nearby. She didn't need much of an explanation, and when she arrived three minutes later, I realized that she might have been keeping a closer eye on us than I'd anticipated.

"Put that away, Chief," she told my stepfather.

"Gladly," he answered as he did as he was told.

As she cuffed Jenkins for the second time that day, she asked Phillip, "Am I correct in assuming that you have a permit for that weapon?"

"It's in my wallet," he said as he started to draw it out.

"That's fine. I don't need to see it," she answered, and then she turned back to her prisoner. "You seem to have a penchant for getting into trouble today, Mr. Jenkins. What am I supposed to do with you?"

"I was minding my own business when these two attacked me!" he screamed. Had that been why he'd been quiet, so he could come up with a story? Surely he didn't think anyone would believe it.

"Let me get this straight. Are you telling me that a donut maker and a senior citizen came after *you*?" she asked incredulously. "Do you really want your buddies down at the bar knowing that they took you down with no muss or fuss?"

He mumbled something, but when she pushed him to repeat it, he refused.

Chief Holmes looked at us. "I'm assuming you want to press charges."

Phillip looked at me. "It's your call, Suzanne."

I thought about doing it out of sheer spite, but then I decided that he wasn't worth the energy. "Will it do any good?" I asked the chief.

"No, I wouldn't think so. He's right. It's your word against his, and he's got the money to pay for a lawyer good enough to get him out of it," she answered candidly.

"Fine. We won't press charges," I said as I took a step toward the man in handcuffs. He actually flinched and took a step backward as I did. It was tough hiding my grin, but I managed somehow. "Is that booze I smell on him?" I asked.

"I thought I smelled something," she said.

"I had one drink!" he shouted. "That's none of your business."

"I'm guessing you had more than one," the chief said, "and if I check at the bar, I'm willing to bet they'll tell me the same thing. After all, you'd *have* to be drunk to rush a cop."

"She's no cop," he said with disdain.

"No, but I am," Phillip answered.

"Mr. Jenkins, you are, at the very least, drunk and disorderly. I think a night in a cell to sleep it off is exactly what you need."

"You can't do that!" he shouted again.

"I can and I will," she answered. "Think about it. You either stay in the jail overnight until you've sobered up, or I'm going to urge these two upstanding citizens to reconsider filing that complaint. Trust me, even if your lawyer can get you off, it's going to cost you."

He stared at her, at us, and then back at the ground. "Fine. Just get me out of here."

"My pleasure," the chief said as she put him in the back of her cruiser yet again.

"Are you sure about not pressing charges?" she asked us after she had him secured.

"I am, but you should tell him if he tries anything else, the next time, we won't bother calling you. We'll handle it ourselves."

"I can't convey a threat like that," she said.

"I understand," I said as I walked over to the car where he was sitting.

After I told him the same thing in person, adding that my husband was also armed around the clock, he settled down pretty quickly. And then I had a sudden thought.

"Why did you follow us here, anyway?" I asked him.

"No reason," he said sullenly.

"You'd better talk, or you won't like what happens next," I warned him. I had no idea what to do if he refused to answer my question, but the open-ended warning was more ominous than a specific threat.

"*He* called me, okay? I owed him one, and he wanted to get rid of you," Jenkins said.

"*Who* called you?" I asked him, noticing that Phillip and Chief Holmes had gotten interested in our conversation.

"*Him*," Jenkins said, gesturing in to the house. "He said that he told you he was getting more booze, but he was calling me as he did it. Like I said, I owed him one, and he decided to collect."

"I think we need to have another conversation with Rudy, don't you?" I asked Phillip.

"I'm right behind you," he said eagerly.

"I might just tag along myself," the chief added.

"What about me? Are you just going to leave me out here alone?"

"You should be fine," she told him. "I'd roll down a window for you, but it's chilly outside, so you'll be okay."

"But I'm cold," he protested.

"Sorry for the inconvenience," she said with a smile, and I liked her at that moment more than I had to date.

There was only one problem when we knocked at the door.

Rudy didn't answer, and with the chief of police right there with us, we couldn't exactly break in.

"How was he when you left him?" the chief asked as she drew her weapon. "Keep that in your holster," she added to Phillip as she saw him start to pull his.

"You need backup," Phillip said.

"No, I don't," she insisted.

He just shrugged, but he made no further move to draw his weapon.

"He was drunk and throwing up in the bathroom," I said.

"So there's a chance he could be in trouble in there?" she asked me. "Is that what you're saying?"

"Yes, and that's the absolute and honest truth," I replied.

"I would think it would be," Chief Holmes said as she tried the doorknob.

It was unlocked.

"I'm going in. Wait here," she told us.

"We can help," I said.

"No, you can't," she answered. "I mean it. Not one step through that doorway. Understand?"

There was no room for debate. "Understood," Phillip and I both said in near unison.

Two minutes later, she came back to the door with her weapon holstered. "You might as well come in."

"What happened to him?" I asked, hoping that I wasn't about to see another dead body.

"I have no idea. He's gone."

"What do you mean, he's gone? That man could barely stagger out of the bathroom, let alone out of the house," I told her.

She took in the scene as we left it, smelling all three glasses. "That's the thing. He wasn't drunk."

"I saw him drink at least a quart of whiskey, and that was while we were here," I told her.

"Smell these glasses," she said, "one at a time."

I leaned over and smelled mine and then Phillip's. "Whiskey in both of them."

"Now smell his," she said.

"It's not whiskey," I replied. Before she could stop me, I dipped a finger in his glass and put it to my lips. "It's sweet tea!"

"He was messing with us?" Phillip asked. "Seriously?"

"Seriously," she said.

"Why would he do that, though, if he weren't guilty of something?" I asked her.

"That's an excellent question, but I'm afraid we'll need to find him to get an answer. Maybe he's doing the same thing you two are doing, trying to find whoever killed Richard Covington."

"Do you think that's possible?" I asked. I had never even considered that as a possibility.

"It's as likely as a crime-fighting donut maker," she said. "Still, I'd like to talk to him to find out if it's true or not."

"What are you doing just standing there, then?" I asked her. The man had played us, and I wasn't all that happy about it, even if it was possible that he was on the side of the angels and trying to find his friend's killer as well. "Put out an APB or something."

"First of all, you don't get to tell me what to do," Chief Holmes said in that professional manner she had about her, "and second of all, he didn't do anything illegal."

"What about lying to us?" I countered.

"You have no official standing in this case. He can lie to you until he's blue in the face. We have no idea *why* he pretended to be drunk, but that doesn't necessarily mean that he's a killer," she said.

"It doesn't exactly paint him as innocent either, does it?" I asked. And then something occurred to me. "Then again..."

"Then again what?" Phillip asked me.

"What if he suspected that whoever killed Richard Covington might be worried about what he told his old friend Rudy before he died? If Rudy was concerned that the killer might come after him next, getting drunk and defenseless would be the *worst* thing he could do. But if he just *pretended* to be drunk, he might just learn the truth."

The chief nodded, and then she turned to Phillip. "She's got a knack for this, doesn't she?"

He agreed. "She's a natural."

"Hey, I'm standing right here, remember?" I told them. "Chief, if you can't even officially look for Rudy, what can you do?"

"I can take care of what I can take care of," she answered. "Mr. Jenkins is going to get himself a nice cell for tonight, and I'm going to keep digging into this murder. What are *you* going to do, Suzanne?"

"Honestly, I think it's time we headed back to April Springs," I told her. "I'm not sure there's anything else we can do here, at least for the moment."

"That sounds like a solid plan to me. If nothing else, it gets you out of my hair for a while," she said. "Let me know when you get back into town, though."

"Why, do you want to catch a bite to eat together, or maybe even see a movie?" I asked her with a smile.

She didn't return it. "I just like knowing what's going on in Maple Hollow," she said. "In the meantime, try to stay out of trouble, would you?"

"Why does everyone keep telling me that?" I asked.

"Maybe because you're so good at it," Phillip answered. "Come on. Your mother made pulled pork for dinner, so if you don't have any plans, I know she'd love to have you eat with us."

"I haven't had a good home-cooked meal in ages," Chief Holmes said wistfully.

"You're more than welcome to join us," I said, knowing that Momma always made way too much of everything.

"I appreciate that, but *someone* has to keep Mr. Jenkins company tonight," she said.

"Don't you have minions for that?" I asked her. Before she could correct me, I added, "Deputies. I meant to say deputies."

"I do, but I can't bring myself to subject them to that," she answered. "Perhaps another time."

"You bet," I said.

When we got back outside, I saw that Mr. Jenkins had slumped down in his seat.

Had the murderer struck again while we'd been inside investigating?

The chief rapped on the window with her knuckle, and Jenkins bolted upright. "What?" he protested.

"Nothing," she replied, clearly relieved that he was okay. "Take care," she told us as she got into her car.

"Right back at you," I said.

Once she was gone, I turned to Phillip. "Are you ready to head home?"

"I am," he admitted. "You're coming with me to dinner, right?"

I thought about that fridge full of delicious leftovers from Napoli's, but then I considered my mother's fresh food. It was a tough decision, but then I realized that I could always eat the goodies from Angelica tomorrow. "If you're sure it's okay."

"I don't even have to let your mother know," he said with a grin. "You *always* have an open invitation at our table."

"Sometimes it pays to have connections," I told him as I started the Jeep, and we headed back into town. It had been a productive trip, but at the moment, we'd covered all of the bases we could. After dinner, I planned on heading back to the cottage and falling asleep on the couch as I watched at least part of the movie I'd mostly slept through the night before.

Without Jake there with me, it was the best I could do, and all in all, it wasn't bad at that.

Chapter 17

I PULLED THE JEEP OVER the second we were out of Maple Hollow's city limits.

"What's going on?" Phillip asked me. "Did you forget something?"

"No. I found something when I was in Rudy's, but I couldn't show you with everything that was happening," I explained as I dug out the envelope.

"Did the chief miss something in Richard's room?" he asked.

"No. This was folded into a towel in the bathroom linen closet," I explained as I gently tore open the seal.

"Wow, you were more thorough than the police," he said in praise.

I wasn't about to admit that I hadn't been snooping but instead searching for a hand towel I could use. "Hey, I have my moments," I said as I carefully opened the flap.

When I turned it over, something tumbled out into my hand.

It was an old coin, and unless I missed my guess, it was the cause of the problem between Paige and the murder victim.

She'd been right.

Richard had had it after all.

"This looks exactly like what Paige suspected," I said as I looked at the coin and then handed it to Phillip.

"Read the letter out loud," my stepfather said as he studied the coin.

I nodded and started to read.

"Dear Paige,

"I wish I could tell you this in person, but you've made it clear that you're done with me, no matter what I have to say. I didn't take the enclosed coin from your home. Whether you believe me or not is out of my hands, but this is the whole truth, no matter how bad it makes my family look. I was honestly puzzled about a great many things that happened in my life, including your family heirloom disappearing, but I was never able

to figure any of it out until my dad died. Mom passed away a few weeks before he did, an odd coincidence if ever there was one, but truly, I think he just couldn't bring himself to live without her.

"He never did have much fight in him.

"Anyway, I was going through his things after the funeral, trying to figure out what to keep, what to sell, and what to give away, when I found a large box hidden away in the back of his closet. Inside it was the most eclectic group of things imaginable, some of great intrinsic value and some barely worth the storage space they took up. Some things I recognized, like my uncle's high school class ring, while others were a complete mystery to me.

"But one item had special significance to me. To us. It was the coin you're holding in your hands right now. It appears my father was a closet kleptomaniac, though he managed to hide it from the world for his entire life. Only in death was his sickness revealed. There was no notebook, no paper trail of any kind to help me figure out where the box of stolen treasures came from. A few I could place, but the rest I ended up donating to a good cause or just discarding altogether.

"That took care of everything he'd stolen over the years but your grandfather's coin. I knew I had to return it to you in person, no matter how painful it would be for me to admit that my father had taken it from your house all those years ago. I needed to see you face-to-face, to share with you the shame and anger I felt at his deceit. I'd wondered even then why he'd volunteered to help 'move some boxes' for your family. When I opened that box, I realized that it was so he could search for something to take, something of value that the owner would miss. It was a particular kind of cruelty doing that, and it breaks my heart to admit it even now.

"I'm going to drop this off at your bookstore in the middle of the night when no one in their right mind is out and about. After you read this letter, please call me, no matter what time it is, day or night. I miss you. You were like a sister to me, and I feel the loss of you in my life every day.

"This is my last resort.

"I have a hunch that once you have this coin in your hands again, I won't get the opportunity to explain anything to you ever again, and I can't let that be the last contact we ever have with each other.

"I guess that's it. I'm giving up and dropping this letter off, along with the coin, as I leave Maple Hollow, April Springs, and North Carolina forever.

"Please know that I am sorry with all of my heart for what my father, and my family, did to you and yours.

"You will always be important to me, no matter how you may feel about me.

"Your next-door neighbor all those years ago, and so very much more than that, a sister of my heart,

"Richie."

"Wow," I said as I let the letter drop into my lap. "Just wow."

"How is Paige going to feel when she reads this?" Phillip asked me.

"She's going to want to die," I told him.

"You must realize that you don't have to give it to her, Suzanne," Phillip said softly.

I looked at him and frowned. "You know that I have to, though, don't you."

"*I* do," he countered. "I just wasn't sure that *you* did. She deserves to know the truth, no matter how much it hurts to hear."

"I'll take care of it," I said, "but I'm going to wait until we figure out who killed Richard Covington."

"Do you think that's wise?" Phillip asked me.

"I'm not doing it for sentimental reasons," I replied. "We might be able to use this to our advantage to flush out Richard's killer," I said as I tapped the envelope.

"That's a little cold and calculating, isn't it?"

I shrugged. "If it is, then so be it. The man deserves justice, and if I have to twist things a bit to make sure he gets it, I can live with that. Can you?"

"I've done worse," Phillip admitted.

"The bad thing is, so have I," I answered as I took the coin from him and put it back into the envelope, along with the letter.

"Do you have a good place to put that in the meantime?" Phillip asked me.

"No, not really. I thought I'd just stick it under the stairs in Jake's hidey hole at the cottage."

"Why don't I put it in our safe for you?" he volunteered.

"You two have a safe?" I asked him, a little surprised. "I figured you two for 'safe deposit box' kind of folks."

"We have those too, but your mother likes to have a few things readily at hand in case she needs them in the middle of the night."

"Do I even want to know what's in there?" I asked him.

"No, and I won't tell you, either. If you want to know that badly, feel free to ask your mother, but that's the most you'll get out of me."

"I believe that is going to be a hard pass," I said. "Thanks. Keep it safe, and when I'm ready for it, I'll ask you for it back," I said as I handed everything to him.

"That's all I ask."

As I started driving again, I asked Phillip, "We don't need to tell anybody about this, do we?"

"Who did you have in mind?"

"Someone in law enforcement," I admitted. "Should Chief Grant or Chief Holmes know about what I found?"

"Do you see it helping their investigation in any way?" he asked me.

"I don't, but then again, I'm biased. *I* don't think Paige had anything to do with Richard Covington's murder."

"Neither do I," he agreed.

"I thought you were the one who said we couldn't cross her name off our list of suspects," I reminded him.

"I did, but that doesn't mean I think she's guilty. I don't see what purpose it would serve to turn this over to the authorities right now. It doesn't exactly clear Paige, does it? As a matter of fact, it could be bad for her."

"How so?" I asked.

"It shows that the two of them were having some serious problems. If they'd found this letter on his body, she'd probably be in jail right now."

"Richard didn't have it with him, though, and I keep wondering what he was doing in April Springs in the middle of the night when he ended up on my donut shop doorstep."

"So do I," he admitted.

"We're walking a fine line here, aren't we?" I asked my stepfather.

"Maybe, but I'm good with it if you are."

"I am. Tell you what, though. If it turns out it looks as though it's relevant, we'll let the proper authorities know about it. Otherwise, we'll save it for Paige for later, after this mess is over and done with."

"I can live with that," Phillip said as he tucked the envelope into his jacket pocket.

My cell phone rang ten minutes from April Springs, and as I glanced at who was calling me, Phillip said, "Eyes on the road, young lady."

"It's Jake," I said, as I swiped to answer it.

Phillip took it and put it on speaker. "Hello, Jake," he said.

"Phillip? Sorry, I meant to call Suzanne," my husband said.

"You did. She's driving at the moment, and I'm in the passenger seat. Sorry, but you've got two for the price of one this evening."

"No worries. How's it going?"

"Good," I said as Phillip said, "Fine," at the same time.

"Okay, one of you at a time. Phillip, as much as I enjoy our little chats, hold the phone out so I can speak with my wife."

"Got it," he said and did as he had been instructed.

"How good is good?" Jake asked me. "Are you two making any progress?"

"We have three solid suspects," I told him.

"Talk to me," Jake said.

"Do you really want to hear all of this? You've got problems of your own."

"Actually, I miss the sound of your voice," he said with a soft chuckle. "That's true, but it's not *just* that. I'm running into a more complicated situation here than I thought I was getting into, so I thought maybe a distraction might be nice."

"So that's all I am to you, a distraction?" I asked him with a hint of laughter in my voice.

"You're more than that, and you know it," he answered, "but I refuse to go into any greater detail with Phillip in the car with you."

"I won't listen," Phillip said as he smiled.

"Liar," we both said simultaneously.

"True enough," Phillip replied.

"So, who are your suspects?" Jake asked.

"As things stand right now, we have Christy Smucker, Richard Covington's once and possibly future girlfriend; Rudy Francis, his friend and rival for Christy's affections; and Geneva Swift, his ex-girlfriend and Momma's assistant."

"Geneva? How did she get mixed up into this?" he asked me.

"She used to date the murder victim, and evidently, they had quite a blowout recently," I said.

"You're forgetting someone, Suzanne," Phillip said gently beside me.

"I gave him all three names on *my* list," I insisted.

"Maybe so, but there are four on mine," he said.

"Who is she leaving out, Phillip?" Jake asked him.

"Paige Hill. She had a history with the vic, and she also had a rather public confrontation with him less than eight hours before he was murdered." Phillip looked at me steadily and added, "I'm sorry, Suzanne, but she can't be ruled out just because she's your friend, even with what we know now."

"I understand that, but I just can't see Paige committing murder, can you?"

"It has been my experience that you never know what people will do when they're pushed hard enough," he said calmly.

"Jake? What do you think?" I asked my husband.

"I'm sorry to say it, but he's right, Suzanne. Paige needs to stay a suspect, at least until you can rule her out logically and not emotionally."

"Fine, gang up on me," I said a bit snippily, and then I added quickly, "Just teasing."

"Are you really, though?" Phillip asked.

"Take my advice and don't push your luck," Jake said. "What are you doing for dinner tonight? Sorry I can't join you."

"Momma made pulled pork," I said a bit too cheerfully.

"Oh, man, now there are *two* reasons I'm sorry I won't be there. First you go to Napoli's without me, and now you're eating at your mother's house," he said, and then I heard someone calling him from a distance. "Yeah, I'll be right there," he told them, and then he added, "Sorry. Gotta go. Love you."

"Love you too," I said.

I wasn't entirely sure whether he had heard my response or not, but I chose to believe that he did.

After Phillip put my phone down, he said, "I didn't mean to imply that I believe Paige is a killer. I just don't think we can discount her until we have more evidence to the contrary."

"It's okay. You're both right. It's something we can't rule out."

"But you still don't think she did it," Phillip said.

"I'd stake my life on it."

"Let's just hope it doesn't come to that," he said as we pulled into their driveway.

Chapter 18

"SUZANNE, I WASN'T EXPECTING you," Momma said when I walked through the door with my stepfather.

"Is it okay that I came?" I asked as I spotted her assistant, and one of our suspects, sitting on the sofa in her living room. "I didn't mean to barge in on anything. I'll catch up with you all later," I turned and said as I headed for the door. "Hey," I told Geneva on the fly.

"Suzanne Hart, stop right there," Momma snapped.

It was a voice I had been trained from birth to obey, and even though I was a grown woman, sometimes it was hard to ignore it when she spoke to me in that tone. "Momma, I..."

She cut me off before I could finish the thought. "You will stay, you will have dinner with us, and you will be pleasant. Is that understood?"

I shrugged. "Would you settle for two out of three?" I asked, trying to laugh it off.

"I will not," she said, refusing to take the peace offering.

"Fine. I'll stay, I'll eat, I'll be nice," I said as I slumped down in a chair like a petulant teen. I hated when I regressed like that, but I couldn't seem to help myself at times.

"Good," she said. "Phillip, I need you in the kitchen."

"Yes, ma'am," he said without a single glance in our direction.

I was alone with a woman I didn't care for, but more than that, she was one of my suspects. Still, even given all of that, I had something I had to do first. I'd promised Paige that I would apologize the first chance I got, and this was clearly that.

"Listen, I want to apologize for siccing Momma on you. I handled that situation poorly, and I'm sorry."

Geneva seemed to be ready for a fight until I confessed, and something went out of her. "It's not your fault. I overstepped my boundaries. Your mother is a wonderful boss, but she has high expectations of me."

"Try being her daughter," I said, warming to the woman despite my feelings for her.

"I can only imagine."

"I'm not sure that you can," I said, "but I'll take it. Are we good?"

"Yes, I am if you are," she said.

"Excellent. I'm glad we got that out of the way. I'm sorry for your recent loss," I said, slipping straight into investigator mode.

"My loss? What do you mean?" she asked. Was she honestly going to try to play innocent with me?

"Richard Covington. I know you two were close, and you wanted to get closer still, so it must have come as a blow to you when he was murdered."

She stiffened so much I thought her back might break. "Richard and I dated briefly a very long time ago. I'm not sure how you know that, which you obviously do, but there is nothing more to it than that."

"Listen, we've all been there," I said, laying it on a little thick. "He was the one who got away, and when he showed up out of the blue, you gave it another shot. No harm in that, but you can't deny that you were with him two nights ago at Napoli's in Union Square. I was there too."

It was a shot in the dark—well, maybe the dusk— but it hit home.

"Have you been spying on me?" she asked as she stood.

"Take it easy. I was there on my own, and I just happened to see you," I said, which was at least partially true. "Why would you deny it if you didn't do anything wrong?"

That set her off again, and her voice got loud enough that I knew I'd pay for it later with Momma, but for the moment I had to push and push hard.

"You are way out of line, Suzanne, and I won't stand for it. Do you hear me?"

"It's a fair question, Geneva, and if you won't answer it coming from me, maybe Chief Holmes will have better luck." It was a ploy to get her to talk to me, one I'd used several times in the past with varying degrees of success, but this time it failed me miserably.

"I'm leaving," she snapped as she grabbed her coat just as Momma and Phillip came out to see what all of the ruckus was about.

"Geneva, where are you going?"

"I suddenly remembered an appointment I need to keep," she said as she stalked toward the door. "Thank you for the invitation, but I really need to go."

"Geneva, stay," Momma said strongly.

"I'm truly sorry, but I really can't," she said, and then she was gone.

"What did you say to her, Suzanne?"

"Hey, I apologized for the way I acted yesterday," I told her.

"She wouldn't have stormed out of here as though the place were on fire if that was *all* that you did, and you know it."

"Okay, maybe I asked her, casually in conversation, about Richard Covington."

Momma looked at me sharply. "The man who was murdered in front of your shop? Why would you ask her about him?" She then turned to her husband. "Phillip, explain."

"We believe Suzanne saw them together at Napoli's the night before he was murdered," he explained.

"Believe? This is all based on supposition?" she asked him critically. "I expect that kind of behavior from her, but you? You were in law enforcement."

My stepfather was usually pretty good about handling my mother, but that crack about his experience was clearly too much for him to take. "That's right, I was. We have more than that. There are witnesses who put them together and even overheard them arguing the night of the murder. She wanted to rekindle their relationship from high school, but it was apparent he was interested in someone else, or maybe none of them at all. You've seen firsthand how the woman behaves around Suzanne. She's got a temper and a bit of a mean streak to boot, and don't deny it."

"She has spirit," Momma said, justifying her assistant's behavior.

"Listen, you can hire and work with anyone you choose, but Suzanne and I are going to figure out who killed that man, one way or the other. If it turns out to have been your assistant, I'm sorry, but I won't back down just because it's inconvenient for you." He then turned to me and said, "Suzanne, I'm sorry I brought you here into this mess. If you want to leave, feel free." Almost as an afterthought, he added, "I might even go with you."

I expected a barrage of anger from my mother when he said that, but evidently he knew what he was doing. His rebellion had been a dash of cold water in her face, and she realized that she had been wrong in attacking his abilities.

"I'm sorry," she said simply, two very powerful words, especially coming from a woman who didn't use them all that often.

"Are you sorry about anything in particular, or is that just a blanket apology?" he asked her with the hint of a smile.

The man was brave, there was no doubt about that, and I didn't know many people who had the nerve to poke the bear like that and expect to get away with it.

"Don't push your luck," she said with a flash of teeth as she gently nudged his chest. I was about to smile when she turned to me. "As for you, you promised to be nice, young lady. I'm disappointed in you."

"Momma, the first words out of my mouth were an apology, and that's the truth."

"Did you push her about the murder?" she asked me.

"Gently," I admitted. "But we can't investigate this by being too cautious and timid around our suspects."

"Do you both honestly believe that I could be that poor a judge of character as to hire someone capable of cold-blooded murder?" Momma asked us.

"Dot, she might be perfect as an assistant, but you can't know what's brewing under the surface. If she felt rejected, she might have done it. Remember Lee Jackson? He was the nicest guy you'd ever want to meet, but when Veronica Bean spurned his advances, he put her in the hospital. You just never know how folks are going to react to being discarded like an old newspaper."

"That was twenty years ago," Momma reminded him.

"So? Does that make it any less valid an argument?" he asked.

"No, I suppose it doesn't. Still, she was a guest in our home."

"That's true, but she *chose* to leave. No one forced her to go," Phillip reminded her gently.

"I truly am sorry, Momma," I said meekly.

"Sorry that you drove her off before you could finish grilling her, or sorry that I'm angry about it?" she asked me.

"Would it be a terrible thing if I admitted that it was a little bit of both?" I asked her.

It was touch and go for a few seconds until she finally shrugged and turned back to the kitchen. "You two are wearying. You know that, don't you?"

"Hey, we have our plus sides too," I reminded her as I smiled at Phillip.

"I know that, but sometimes..."

I didn't want her to finish that sentence, and I was sure that her husband didn't want her to, either.

I took a deep breath. "That smells amazing. You're still going to feed me, right?"

Momma studied me for a moment, and then she broke out a smile. "Have I *ever* refused you?"

I decided to let that one go. After all, I didn't have to swing at every pitch I got. "Excellent. Let's eat, then," I said, ignoring her question.

"Sounds good to me," Phillip said, and then he gave my mother a quick kiss. "Are we good?"

"We are golden," she said as she led us into the dining room.

"That was incredible," I told her after finishing the meal. I'd chosen wisely. As good as the leftovers from Napoli would surely be, this was special too. Momma had outdone herself, and I felt a twinge of remorse for depriving Geneva Swift of the experience.

But it was just a twinge.

I wasn't finished with that woman yet, no matter how it might upset Momma.

After all, if she had indeed killed Richard Covington, she had to pay for her crime, even if it did inconvenience my mother by robbing her of her new assistant.

I was tired by the time dessert was over, a wonderful chocolate lava cake that exploded with flavor the moment it hit my tongue, so I decided that it was time to go.

As they both walked me to the door, I asked, "Will I see you in the morning, Phillip?"

To his credit, he didn't even glance at my mother. "I'm going to see this to the end, with or without you."

"I feel the same way," I said. "Come by the shop at eleven, and we can get started again."

"I'll see you then," he said. "Now if you ladies will excuse me, I'm going to get another piece of that amazing cake."

"Make it a small one," Momma said.

"I can try, but I'm not making any promises. If you don't want me indulging, then maybe you shouldn't do such a good job feeding me," he said as he kissed her cheek.

Once he was gone, Momma said, "My husband has grown rather deft in handling me, hasn't he?"

Wow, was that a minefield. There was no way I could win by answering or even acknowledging that question. "Yeah, it's getting cooler outside. We might get snow soon if this keeps up."

Momma smiled. "Well done, Suzanne. Take care of him, would you? And while you're at it, be careful yourself. I love you both too much to let anything happen to either one of you."

"We feel the same way about you, Momma," I said as I hugged her, something that always gave me a bit of peace in a world with so little of it. "Good night."

"Good night, dear child," she said.

By the time I got home, I was feeling pretty good about my life. A full belly and a warm hug would do that to me, and even though I missed my husband, all was pretty right with the world.

And then I spotted two shadows creeping up onto my porch.

As my headlights hit them, they froze in place, and I slammed the Jeep into park and rushed out to confront them.

Chapter 19

"WHAT DO YOU TWO THINK you're doing?" I asked as they stood there, too shocked by being caught to even try to run away. I knew them both, so it wouldn't do them any good, so maybe that was what kept them rooted to their spots.

When there was no answer, I said, "Gary Thrush, Billy Knight, you two are both too old to be pulling pranks on me."

They had both been customers of mine for years, since they were in-nocent little boys excited to get my donuts. They had grown into brash teenagers now, though, and it was difficult to see the sweet little boys they'd been while they carried a withered old funeral wreath between them.

"Ms. Hart, we weren't expecting to see you here," Gary said. He'd always been the ringleader, with Billy doing just about anything his friend suggested.

"That's pretty obvious, isn't it?" I asked as I approached them. "First the cross, and now this. Explain." When they were quiet for too long, I pulled out Momma's tone of voice that always chilled me to the core. "You can answer me, or you can answer the police," I said as I reached for my cell phone. I had no intention of calling Chief Grant or anyone else on his staff, but they didn't have to know that.

"It was just a goof," Billy said timidly.

"Billy," Gary warned him.

"No, I'm not going to let you steamroll me anymore, Gary," he protested before he turned back to me. "Somebody bet us we didn't have the stones to play a prank on you. We shouldn't have done it, and we're sorry." When his cohort didn't respond, Billy nudged him. "Right?"

"Right," Gary said, though it was pretty clear he was uncomfortable with this new dynamic.

"What are you going to do to us, Ms. Hart? Please don't call the cops. Dad said if I got caught doing anything else stupid, he'd take away my phone." I knew for a kid his age, that was as close to capital punishment as it usually got.

"I won't call them," I said, and the relief on their faces was obvious. A little too obvious for my taste.

"Don't think you're getting away with this, though. You are both banished from Donut Hearts for the rest of your natural lives," I said, trying to make it sound as though I was delivering the death penalty.

Their faces both went white, and I knew that I'd struck home. "For life? Come on, we didn't mean anything by it," Billy pled.

Even Gary was upset by the verdict. "What am I going to tell my folks? I pick up the donuts every Saturday, and if I say I can't, they're going to kill me."

Did he honestly think I'd forgotten that particular fact? These boys were scared, but I realized that the punishment outweighed the crime. "I might reconsider," I said.

"We'll do anything," Gary replied.

I thought about it a second, and then I had it. "You can wash the windows of my shop first thing tomorrow morning, and they need to be spotless," I told them. The looks on their faces told me that they knew they were getting off easy, maybe a little too easy, especially since there was just one large window and a glass door to my place. "And The Last Page too," I added.

"Really? But there has to be a hundred windows there," Gary protested.

"Probably not more than twenty," I said, "but you need to make a choice. If those windows aren't clean by ten thirty tomorrow morning, don't bother coming back to Donut Hearts again."

"We'll be there at seven," Gary said.

"Six," Billy corrected him, and the two started to slink away into the park.

"Boys, aren't you forgetting something?" I asked. As they turned, I pointed to the discarded funeral wreath, as well as the makeshift cross, which they had found and propped back up on my door again.

"Sorry," they both said as they retrieved their offerings.

"Who put you up to it?" I asked them.

Billy answered without hesitation. "Like I said, we were just being stupid, but we're not going to rat anyone out. If you want to ban us, then go ahead, but nobody put a gun to our heads."

Gary was about to protest when his friend caught his eye. Wow, it was crazy to see how their relationship had changed right in front of my eyes. I doubted Gary would ever push Billy again.

"I understand that, but give them a message for me, would you?" I asked sweetly.

"We can do that," Billy conceded.

"My husband goes around armed, and he might not take kindly to someone trespassing. It's not a threat, though. Think of it more as a warning. There are consequences to your actions, some you might not realize at the time."

Wow, when had I become my mother? She'd used those exact words on me when I'd been younger, and they'd certainly made an impression on me.

Those kids couldn't get out of my presence fast enough, and I had a feeling that I wouldn't be having any more problems with people leaving things on my doorstep anymore.

That solved a minor problem, but I had something much bigger on my plate, and at the moment, I had no idea what the answer might be.

All I could say for sure was that I would keep digging until I got to the truth, no matter where it might lead me.

And that included Paige Hill's front door.

I reached for Jake the moment I woke up the next morning, and it took me half a second to remember that he was gone. I hated our separations, but I knew that it was important, if not vital, for him to have his own life. He'd tried retirement, and it hadn't worked out for him. Now that he'd found a purpose, he was his old self again. If that meant that I had to spend time away from him, then so be it. His happiness was all that really mattered to me.

I checked the fridge for something to eat for breakfast and decided to have some of my leftovers from Napoli's. Lasagna might not be most folks' idea of a great breakfast, but then chances were good that they hadn't had Angelica's delightful food.

I made it to the shop with time to spare, and as I prepped for another day of making donuts, I had time alone to come up with our next move in our investigation. Having that first hour alone had become important to me again, and I relished the chance to work in the silence. As I prepped the batter for the cake donuts, I considered what had worked for me in my past investigations. Some of my strategies were out, but when I thought about what I had to work with on this case, it suddenly became clear to me.

I couldn't be passive anymore and wait for the clues to come to me.

I had three—four if you asked Phillip—solid suspects, and there didn't seem to be a great deal of hope waiting for one of them to slip up.

It was time to take action, and that meant setting a trap.

By the time Emma came in an hour later, I had a good plan. At least I thought it would work. I'd have to run it past Phillip after work before we implemented it, but I believed it would have a very good chance of succeeding. What was more, if I was right, by nightfall, we could very possibly know who killed Richard Covington.

"Morning, Suzanne," Emma said as she came into the kitchen and grabbed her apron a minute before four a.m. "Wow, those smell amazing. I never get tired of the aroma of freshly made donuts, do you?"

"It's something I take for granted some days, but I love it too. What does Barton think about you smelling like donuts all of the time?"

"He loves it!" she said, laughing. "I was lucky enough to find a boyfriend who thinks fried dough is one of the essential aromas in life."

"You are at that," I said as I kept dropping donut batter into the fryer. "How is the restaurant coming? Will you be ready for the grand opening?"

"I don't see how," she said with a frown. "Whoever knew that opening a restaurant would entail so much work? Between here, my classes, and Barton, I barely have time to turn around."

I was hoping she wasn't leading up to something, like resigning from Donut Hearts, but in the back of my mind, I always knew that it was a possibility. Maybe I could nip it in the bud. "If you need to take a little time off, I'd be happy to take the shop over again. Without the responsibility of running the place two days a week, you might have more time."

"You're not unhappy with what Mom and I are doing, are you?" she asked me.

"No, of course not. I was just trying to make life easier for you."

"Then don't take away my two days here," she said with a grin. "Running Donut Hearts part-time is the only thing that's keeping me sane. I feel as though it's something I can control, as opposed to the rest of my life."

"I get that. I was just trying to help."

"Believe me, you're the least of my worries," she told me as she dove into the dishes. "Any news on Richard Covington?" she asked casually.

"No," I said.

"Hey, I wasn't prying. I was just curious. That's all."

"I didn't mean to be so short with you, but I really don't have anything new to report. We're having trouble nailing things down. We haven't even tried asking folks for their alibis. Who has a good one in the middle of the night?"

"Not me," she said. "I can see where that could be a problem."

"Let's not think about bad things," I suggested.

"I agree. Hey, I saw a poster for Max's new play. What a hoot that's going to be. Are you going?"

"I extorted four free tickets from him in exchange for donuts weeks ago," I told her with a grin. "Jake promised to take me, and we're going to invite Grace and Stephen too."

"And if they can't make it?" she asked.

"Momma and Phillip, I suppose. Why?"

She hesitated a moment and then said, "If you can't find anyone to go with you, Barton and I would love to."

"I figured you two would be too busy with what was on your plates," I said.

"We are, but sheesh, he hasn't taken me anywhere but competitors and restaurant supply houses for months. I could use a little romancing, you know?"

I laughed. "Welcome to the world of serious relationships. Tell you what. If Grace and Steven can't make it, you'll be next in line."

"I wouldn't want to bump your mother," she said. "I have no problem being part of the third couple on your list."

"Good enough," I said. As I pulled the last cake donut out of the oil, I added, "Once the restaurant opens...nothing's probably going to change."

"Wow, what words of hope and inspiration," she said with a laugh. "If you'll excuse me, I think I'll go out front and step in front of a bus."

"There hasn't been a bus through here in twenty years since they moved the depot to Union Square, but if you don't mind waiting, go right ahead."

"Is it really going to be that bad?"

"You two will figure it out. I have faith in you, but you're a grown woman, Emma. You have to think of yourself as a partner, and I don't mean just in business." I realized that I was giving her the same speech Momma had given me before I'd married Max, and look how that had turned out. "And thus ends the lecture. Don't forget about the pop quiz on Friday, and your special projects are due by the end of the month."

She smiled at me. "I won't, Teach."

Chapter 20

WHEN I OPENED THE DOOR for business, I was surprised to see two faces there that I hadn't been expecting until much later.

I stepped outside into the chill morning air and said, "Guys, you're *way* too early. Can you even see the windows enough to wash them?" I asked Gary and Billy.

"We brought a spotlight with us," Billy said with a smile. He turned it on, and it lit up the front of my shop, it was so bright.

Emma came out to see what was going on. "Who ordered the Bat Signal?" she asked.

"I've got this covered. These gentlemen have kindly volunteered to wash our front window and the door," I told her.

She looked at them and then back at me. "Okay. Whatever. I'm going to get back to work."

Once she was gone, Billy asked me, "Is she dating anybody?"

"She's too old for you, and besides, she's out of your league," Gary answered.

"Maybe so, but if I don't ask, how will I ever know?" he replied with a smile.

"True enough. Go for it, dude."

"Sorry to break it to you, but she's dating someone," I said.

"Is it serious?" he asked.

I thought about encouraging him to ask her out anyway, but I couldn't do it to the poor kid. "Very."

He took it in stride. "Understood. Can we get some water, Ms. Hart? We've got everything else we need."

"There's a tap in back," I said. "Ordinarily I'd show you where it is, but with that signal beam of yours, you won't have any trouble finding it."

They nodded and took off around the side of the building.

The teens got points not only for showing up when they said they would but also for having a good attitude about it. I knew that some apples were just plain bad—I'd seen enough of that to last me a lifetime—but these were just kids without a malicious bone in their bodies.

Well, not many, anyway.

As I sold donuts for the next half hour, several people asked about what was going on out front. I told them I was giving a pair of entrepreneurs a chance and left it at that. There was no reason to go into the backstory of why they were really there.

"We're finished here," Billy said as he and Gary came into the shop after inspecting their work one last time. I'd been watching them work, both inside and out, and they had done an extremely thorough job on both sides of the glass.

"Everything looks great," I said as I grabbed them each a donut and a hot chocolate.

"What's this for?" Billy asked.

"Consider it a tip," I told them as I set them up.

"We should be doing *you* a favor," Billy said with enthusiasm.

"We've got three jobs lined up cleaning windows on Saturday," Gary chimed in. "Thanks for sending customers our way."

"I didn't mean to back you both into a corner," I said, apologizing.

"Are you kidding? We can earn enough to rent fancy tuxes, and maybe even a limo too, for the prom," Billy said.

"That sounds good, but don't forget, this was just the first part of our agreement," I said as I pointed toward the bookstore across the street.

"We'll take care of it," Gary said. "You can count on us."

"You know what? I believe I can."

Two minutes after Paige showed up at the bookshop, she headed toward Donut Hearts. I'd been keeping an eye on The Last Page, so I was ready when she got there.

"I understand I have you to thank for my windows being washed this morning," she said with a grin. "Care to tell me the reason?"

"Do you really need to know?" I asked her, returning her smile. "Just accept it with grace and dignity."

"We both know that's not going to happen," she laughed.

I told her what had happened.

"I like your sense of justice," Paige said. "And I appreciate the work. Should I tip them?"

"I gave them donuts and hot chocolate," I told her.

"Well, I can't top that," she said.

"You could let them each pick out a book," I suggested.

"That could get pricy."

"I've got an idea. Surely they've worked up more of an appetite by now. Take them more donuts and hot chocolate, and I'm sure they'll be delighted."

She looked at the case. "Are you sure you have them to spare?"

"Trust me, I'm going to have at least three dozen left over if things stay the way they are." As I got the order together, I asked, "How are you doing?"

"Terrible," she admitted. "I barely slept at all last night. I can't believe what a jerk I was to Richard. We were as close as a brother and a sister could be, and all because of one stupid thing he did, I shut him out of my life forever. I always thought we'd get past it someday, but that's never going to happen now."

I thought about telling her about the letter and the coin, but I couldn't do it.

At least not just yet.

Then I thought about Phillip and how he'd insist that I set the trap for Paige as well as our other suspects. I just couldn't bring myself to do that yet either, especially since my partner hadn't approved of my plan yet.

Who was I kidding? I didn't do it because I still couldn't bring myself to believe that Paige had killed Richard Covington.

"Suzanne, are you sure I can't pay you for these?" she asked as she took the order.

"We're good," I said. "I would like to touch base with you later, though."

"I've got a minute right now," she said as she looked at her watch. "What's up?"

"Sorry, but it needs to be later," I insisted.

"Fine," she said, her light spirit dimmed for a moment. "Thanks again."

"You're very welcome," I told her.

Paige glanced back at me one more time before she left, and I knew that she could read my expression. I was troubled, and there was no hiding it.

I just hoped that she didn't know why.

That wasn't all, though. There had been something in her face as well that had bothered me.

Was it possibly even guilt over what she'd done?

I hated thinking about my friend that way, but I couldn't help myself.

One way or the other, I was going to have to end this or risk losing a dear friend, even if she wasn't a cold-blooded killer.

Two minutes before I was set to close, the last person on earth I expected to see came into the donut shop.

"Hello, Geneva. Listen, I'm sorry about last night..."

She wouldn't even let me get through my apology. "I'm here to say that I'm sorry for the way I behaved, and I'll cooperate with you and Phillip in any way I can."

I studied her a moment before commenting. "Did Momma put you up to that?"

It was obvious that she had, but my question was, would Geneva admit it? "She thought it best if we could work out our differences."

"So that's a yes," I said.

"It doesn't matter. What can I do for you?"

At least the shop was empty of other customers. "First things first. Did you kill Richard Covington?"

"Seriously? You're actually asking me that?" she said, her calm demeanor slipping away entirely for a moment. That was the temper I'd seen just below the surface, but it wasn't hiding any more.

"It's a fair question. He rejected you, and you reacted. It has been known to happen before."

"I didn't kill anyone!" she said.

"Honestly, I don't even know why I asked you that," I said, making a sudden and executive decision. I hadn't gone over my plan with Phillip yet, but it was time to strike. "I'll know tonight who killed him, anyway."

"What? How is that even possible?" she asked, her face growing a bit taut.

I looked around, pretending as though I was sharing vital information. "Just between you and me, I lied to the police. To everyone, really."

"You did?" she asked, clearly shocked by my admission. "How so?"

"Richard said something to me just before he died."

"He what?" she practically shouted.

Emma poked her head out of the kitchen. Evidently she'd heard Geneva's outburst even over her music as she did dishes. "Is everything okay out here?"

"It's fine, Emma," I told her.

After a second, she ducked back into the kitchen.

"What did he tell you?" Geneva asked once she was gone, "and why didn't you tell anybody?"

"It didn't make sense at the time," I told her. "I just figured it out ten minutes ago."

"Suzanne, you need to tell me. I have a right to know."

I wasn't at all sure that was the case, but it was my plan to get her curious about what I'd heard or least what I was about to claim I heard. "He whispered, "The dog's guarding it. Loose brick. Check the dog.""

"He had time to whisper that but not to name his killer?" she asked.

Now that I thought about it, it was a reasonable question. Why *hadn't* he told me a name if I were telling the truth? It was time to improvise. "Think about it. He'd been stabbed in the back of the neck and clobbered with something hard in the head. He obviously wasn't thinking clearly," I said, and as I did, I believed it, playing out the scenario in my mind. I'd had a concussion once after falling off my bicycle, and Momma told me that I'd muttered something about how the moose was loose ten minutes after it happened, whatever that was supposed to mean.

"What does it even mean, though?"

"I didn't know either, but when Phillip and I were in Maple Hollow yesterday, I couldn't help seeing the mascot's statue in front of the high school."

"Our bulldog," she said as she shook her head. "Is that what you think he meant?"

"Think about it. It's on a brick pedestal, and given the shape it's in, it's not hard to imagine one of the bricks is loose. If Richard was trying to hide something in plain sight, what better place to do it than that?"

"I suppose so," she said. "Are you going to go see what he hid there?"

Good. It appeared that she was buying my story. Now for the clincher.

"I am, but I can't do it for a few hours. I called Chief Holmes, and she insists that she meet Phillip and me there. We were told in no uncertain terms not to go anywhere near that statue until she was with us.

Thanks for coming by, though. I'll try to be nicer to you from here on out. I know it's not easy doing what you do."

"I will make more of an effort myself," she said as she left, nearly running Phillip down in her haste to get out of there.

"What's going on?" Phillip asked me. "She looked as though she just saw a ghost."

"She might have at that," I said. "Emma!" I called out.

"Yes, Boss?" she answered.

"Close up, okay?"

"You got it."

"Where are we going in such a hurry?" I asked him.

"Maple Hollow. We're going to catch a killer today."

Chapter 21

AS WE DROVE, I CAUGHT Phillip up on my plan.

After I finished, he said, "You really should have spoken to me about it first, Suzanne."

"I know, but there wasn't time. I figure we'll go see Christy, try to find Rudy, and then stake out the statue to see who shows up."

"That's not going to work," he said with a frown.

"Why not?"

"Someone needs to guard that statue the second we get to town," Phillip said. "I'm armed, so I'll do it."

"Why shouldn't I?" I asked him stubbornly.

"You need to talk to the others to finish setting the trap," he said, "and you need to do it in person, except for one suspect."

"Which one is that?" I asked, knowing full well who he was talking about.

"Call Paige and give her the same setup you're feeding the others," he said.

"That means that I have to think she could have done it," I protested, even though that wasn't true, and what was more, I knew it. It just felt disloyal somehow setting up my friend.

"Think of it this way. It gives her a chance to prove me wrong," he answered. "Go on. I'll even dial the number for you."

"Fine, I'll do it, but not another word from you. Agreed?"

"Agreed," he answered as he hit her name in speed dial and then put it on speaker so he could hear as well.

After the trap was set, I made a kill gesture, and he ended the call on our end. "Satisfied?" I asked him a bit petulantly.

"Suzanne, I don't like this any more than you do, but we have to know."

The pain in his voice was obvious, and I felt an instant pang of remorse for my attitude. "I know. You're right. I'm sorry."

"Six words I never thought I'd hear from a woman in my life, all strung together," he said, flashing a grin to show me that there were no hard feelings.

"Relish them then, because I'm not about to repeat them," I answered. "So, what's our new plan?"

"Drop me off near the statue, and I'll find a place to stake it out. Then go find Christy and Rudy if you can, and tell them the same story. After that, park the Jeep out of sight and come looking for me. How does that sound to you?"

"It's as good a plan as we can come up with on the fly. I'm sorry I pulled the trigger without you," I added.

"No worries, Suzanne. You saw an opportunity, and you seized it. I would expect nothing less of you."

"I appreciate that," I answered.

We got close to the abandoned high school and the statue I'd used as a lure, and Phillip waved me over to the side of the road. "I'll walk the rest of the way from here. Be careful," he said.

"Right back at you. See you soon."

Once I was on my own, I had to decide which suspect to visit first. I wanted to give Phillip all of the time I could to get himself set up, so I decided to go to Rudy's place first. Chances were good that he was long gone, so when I spoke to Christy, I'd have a chance to rush back to the statue and wait with Phillip for someone to show up.

There was just one problem with that, though.

Rudy was home, and when he answered his front door, I was surprised to find Christy Smucker there with him as well.

It appeared that I was about to kill two birds with one stone.

"Suzanne, what are you doing here?" Rudy asked me, clearly surprised by my visit.

"I could ask you the same thing," I told him. "Hey, Christy."

"Hello. I just came by to talk to Rudy. He told me that the fight with Jenkins out front shook him up yesterday, so he took off out the back door until things settled down," she explained. Why she thought I needed to know that was beyond me, but then she added, "By the way, I didn't stay here last night."

I had a feeling that she'd done just that, but it really wasn't any of my business. "Hey, you are two grown people. You can do what you want," I said a little flippantly.

"Yeah, and if you don't mind, we'd like to get back to it," Rudy said, keeping me from coming in.

Ordinarily I wouldn't have dreamed of intruding, but this wasn't a social call. "This will just take a second. There's an update on Richard's murder case I thought you might like to know."

Before Rudy could shut the door in my face, Christy stepped into the frame. "Come in. Of course we want to know."

Rudy didn't look pleased that I'd interrupted them, but he had no choice at that point. "Sure, come on in. The more the merrier."

I went inside, but I stayed close to the door, just in case. I felt better with both of them there, but I realized that it was possible that they might have killed Richard together. Had the stories I'd gotten from them earlier been smokescreens? If they'd lied to us or the folks around them had misunderstood their relationship, I might have just walked into a hornet's nest without meaning to.

"You know what? I'll come back later," I said as I suddenly felt a chill sweep through me. Why had I come there alone? I knew better, but it had seemed harmless enough at the time. It was hard to believe that ten minutes earlier, I'd thought that Phillip had been taking all of the risks, not me.

"Stay," Christy insisted as she stepped between me and my escape route. "Talk."

I looked at Rudy, who just shrugged. "You might as well tell us. She's not going to let you leave until you do."

If even then, I realized. It was time to make a choice. I could either come up with something else on the fly, or I could bull my way through our original plan. I decided that Christy wouldn't make a move on me with Rudy there—unless they had conspired to kill Richard Covington together.

If that was the case, there was a good chance that there wasn't any hope left for me.

"When Richard died, he whispered something to me that sounded like nonsense," I told them, doing my best to sell it. "It took me until an hour ago to figure it out."

"What did he say?" Christy asked insistently as she got closer and closer to me. I looked from her to Rudy, who was taking a few steps back. "Did he say anything about me?"

Was that a confession to murder? I had to stall her, and fast, to keep her from acting. "No, he didn't mention anyone in particular," I said quickly. "He said something about a dog guarding a clue about who attacked him and mentioned loose bricks. I had no idea what he was saying, given that he probably had a concussion and was dying, but then I remembered the bulldog statue at the high school. I was on my way to check it out with the police chief later when I thought you might want to hear about it first."

"She's meeting you there?" Christy asked insistently.

"No, it won't be until later. I have a few other things to do in town, and she forbade me from going there without her. I won't be able to go for a few hours myself." I did my best to sell it, but it was pretty clear that Christy wasn't buying it. "I'm going to swing by Burt's and get something to eat. You two want to come with me while I wait?"

It was weak, and I really wasn't surprised that nobody bought it.

I was in trouble, and I knew it.

I had thought Rudy was distancing himself from us so he could let Christy handle me, but when he spoke next, I saw that something else had been happening all along while I'd been distracted by her.

Rudy held a handgun, and he was pointing it at us both as he said, "Step away from her, Christy."

Chapter 22

I WASN'T SURE WHO WAS more confused, Christy or me.

"Rudy, what are you doing? She's trying to help us find Richard's killer." Christy protested.

"That's not what she's doing here at all," Rudy said. "She knows who did it, or at least she has a pretty good idea. If she gets that proof and gives it to the cops, it's going to be all over."

"Isn't that a good thing?" Christy asked, clearly puzzled by Rudy's abrupt change in behavior.

"Not if you're the one who killed him," he said coolly.

"Rudy! I didn't do that! I would never!"

"Yeah, well, you didn't have to, because I took care of him myself," he said.

And that was the confession that counted.

"Why would you kill him?" she asked, a pleading in her voice that was heartbreaking.

"You didn't love him. You love me," he said.

"I don't, well, at least, not like that," she replied.

The words hit him hard, but he tried not to show it. "Then why did you spend the night here last night?"

"I needed someone to comfort me," she said. "I can't believe you would do such a horrible thing." Christy looked at him as though he were some kind of bug that repulsed her.

"I did it for you. For us. Now we can be together," he said.

I started to inch toward the door, hoping that Rudy was too distracted by being rejected, but sadly, that wasn't the case. "Stay right there or I'll end you, Suzanne. I'm not bluffing."

He wasn't, either. I could hear it in his voice. I was going to have to do something, but I didn't know what it might be. If I didn't, I knew without a shadow of a doubt that I'd soon be joining Richard Covington in the morgue.

Christy stared at him in disgust. "You're nothing but a common murderer. I could *never* be with you."

The clarity she said it with was so strong that there was no doubt in my mind that Rudy had played his cards all wrong.

"You don't mean that," he said, trying to cajole her as though she were a baby.

"I've never meant anything more in my life," she said.

"You'll come around. Just give it some time, and you'll see that we belong together."

This man was seriously deluded if he thought she'd change her mind.

"I won't," she said firmly.

"You just need to think about it." He ripped the cord off the closest blinds and threw it to me. "Tie her up."

"What? I'm not going to help you," I told him.

"Do it, or I'll shoot you, and then I'll do it myself."

I took the cord as he motioned Christy to a dining-room chair. As I started to do as he'd instructed, he added, "Make it tight, or you won't see the outside ever again."

There went that plan. As I knelt down to tie her, I whispered, "I'm so sorry."

"It's not your fault," she replied.

"No talking!" Rudy shouted, showing some of the craziness he had lurking just below the surface.

I finished the job, and then Rudy waved me over to the closet. "Stand over there and don't move."

I did as I was told, and he quickly checked the bindings. As he leaned toward her, I heard Christy plead, "Don't do this, Rudy. Nobody else has to die."

"Not if everyone does as they are told, they don't," he said. Once he was confident in the job I'd done, he told her almost gently as he stroked her hair lightly, "Don't try to get free." He took her cell phone and tucked it into his pocket as he added, "If you manage to get yourself free, I'll find you, and you won't be happy about it. Neither will your mother." The threat was very real.

Her face lost all color. "I won't do anything."

"That's a good girl," he said as he patted her head as though she were a toddler. After Rudy stood, he turned to me. "Come on."

"Where are we going?" I asked.

"We're going to go see what Richard hid in the statue base. I've got a hunch I know what it is, and we need to grab it before the police chief does."

He had believed my bluff after all.

Maybe there would be a chance of me getting out of this alive after all.

Just maybe.

As we got into my Jeep, he jammed the gun into my ribs. "Don't get any ideas, Suzanne. Drive slowly to the statue and park in front of it. If you try to wreck us or drive us into a tree, you'll be dead before you can do anything, and I'll take my chances. Understand?"

I'd done just that in the past, but this time, I wanted to make it to our destination. After all, I had one more surprise for him.

Phillip was waiting, and with any luck, we'd get through this after all.

As I drove, slower than I normally would, I asked, "I know why you killed him, and how, but why do it in April Springs? How did you even lure him there in the middle of the night?"

"It was easy as pie. I stole Christy's phone and used it to get him there. I couldn't very well kill him in Maple Hollow. That might be too easy to trace back to me. No, I needed a fall guy. In this case, it was going to be a fall gal."

I got it. "You told him to meet you at the bookstore so you could point the finger at Paige Hill."

"It would have worked, too, if he hadn't been so stubborn about dying when he should have. I had this gun with me, but it was going to be a last resort. Shooting it in the middle of the night would have gotten me more attention than I wanted. I shoved that ice pick into the back of his neck, and I thought for sure it would kill him instantly, but he fought back. I hit him in the back of the head with a rock, and the fool still wouldn't die! He even hit me back! It took me a second to get my bearings, and by the time I could come after him to finish the job once and for all, he was already at your donut shop. It was the only light around, and when I looked inside, I saw you and that cop rushing out to help him. I hid back in the shadows, wondering if I was going to have to shoot all three of you and risk the noise, when I realized that he'd finally died. I never dreamed he'd be that tough to kill."

"Did you really think Christy would just accept what you did?" I asked him as we neared the statue.

"She will. I can convince her. I'm sure of it," he said as he looked around at the deserted school, along with the forlorn bulldog statue. "I told Richard that *I* was in love with her, but he didn't care! He mocked me, and I knew that I had to get rid of him. The fool sealed his own fate when he stole my girlfriend. He deserved what he got."

"I thought he was going to break up with her," I pointed out.

"Yeah. I lied about that. They were going to run away together, and I couldn't have that."

"What do you think he hid?" I asked, hoping to learn if there was something out there that might implicate him after all.

"It's probably a letter I was writing Christy when Richie was staying with me. I told her that I'd do anything to be with her, even kill for her. I decided that wasn't the right approach, so I crumpled it up and threw it away, but he must have dug it out of the trash to use against me. Once I have that back, I'll be able to do what I want."

I decided not to remind him that Christy and I had both heard his confession. He had more loose ends than he was willing to address, at least for now.

"Give me the keys," he said as I stopped where he'd pointed.

I did as he said and got out.

"Slowly," Rudy cautioned me.

I moved more deliberately, trying not to look around for Phillip. He was out there. I was sure of it.

Rudy quickly joined me and jammed the gun into my back, making me yelp a little. "Come on. I don't have all day. Get it."

"I don't know exactly which brick to check," I told him.

What was Phillip waiting for? Did he not have a shot, or was he afraid of hitting me instead? If he didn't do something quickly, it was going to be too late.

It was beginning to feel as though I was going to have to save myself.

I reached down and pretended to pry at a place on the statue base when I picked up a nearby brick that had fallen from the top. There was a scrap of paper near it, a torn flyer about a lost dog. "This must be it," I said as I stood.

I had enough space for that split second to swing the brick at him when his focus went to the paper, and I did it with all of my might.

Rudy must have sensed my plan, though, and I heard the gun go off.

By some miracle, the first shot missed me completely.

I knew that the second one wouldn't, though.

As I swung the brick toward his head a second time, he swung his gun hand around, and I shifted my focus to that instead. The brick hit his hand, not the gun, but it still scored, and the weapon went flying.

I dove for it, but Rudy was too quick for me.

He grabbed me from behind, and before I could reach the handgun, he had his hands around my throat and started choking the life out of me.

Chapter 23

THE NEXT THING I KNEW, Phillip was on Rudy's back, his own weapon pressed against the man's head. "Let her go right now, or you die." There was a calm certitude to him that spoke more than a shout would have managed.

He meant business.

Rudy pulled his hands away, and I scrambled out from under him. As Phillip bound his hands with the large zip ties he'd had with him for just that purpose, I rubbed my neck and said, "Not that I'm not grateful, but what took you so long?"

"I couldn't get a clear shot at him," he said, clearly frustrated. "If I'd tried to take him out, I could have hit you, and your mother would have killed me if I'd shot her only daughter."

There was nothing funny about the situation, but his explanation made me laugh nonetheless. Phillip grinned and shrugged at the same time when Rudy said, "You two are crazier than I am."

"There's no doubt about it," Phillip answered as he pulled out his cell phone.

Chief Holmes must have been nearby, because she was there in minutes. I caught her up on what had happened, including the confession and the kidnapping. That was when I remembered Christy Smucker, still tied up and waiting in Rudy's living room.

"I'll send someone over there right now," the chief said after I told her. "You need to come to the station with me so we can write this all up."

"I'd be glad to," I said. "I need to get my keys back, though. They're in his pocket." I could barely bring myself to look at our captive, let alone touch him.

"I'll take care of that," she said as she glanced at Phillip. "Cover me."

"With pleasure," my stepfather said.

Rudy started to squirm, and the chief asked, "Do you really want to do that? I can make things considerably worse for you than they are right now. If you move again, you'll be limping to the car."

"You're going to let him shoot me?" Rudy asked, clearly a little crazed.

"Of course not," she answered pleasantly. "I'll do it myself."

After that, Rudy cooperated, and soon, I was following the police chief's car to the station. It hadn't exactly ended like we'd planned, but we'd caught a killer, and in the end, that had been our ultimate goal.

It wouldn't bring Richard Covington back, but at least his killer would pay for the crime.

It was the best we could do for him at that point.

And then I remembered the coin and the letter back at Phillip's place.

Chapter 24

"SO HE NEVER TOOK IT after all," Paige said later as she read the letter on the front steps of her bookstore. She kept playing with the coin with her free hand as though it were some kind of talisman. "I can't believe how wrong I was."

"You can't be too hard on yourself," I told my friend. "We all do things we regret."

"Even you?" she asked me as the tears tracked gently down her cheeks.

I had debated on sharing the next bit of information with her, but now I knew that I had no choice. "Paige, until today, you were on our list of suspects. I'm sorry."

"Don't be," she said as she put the coin away and wiped the tears with her now free hand. "You had to do what you thought was right."

"You're not upset with me?" I asked her, the relief flowing through me.

"Am I happy you thought I could be a killer? No, of course not. But you said all along that you were going to find out who killed Richard, no matter what, and that's exactly what you did. Suzanne, thank you."

I never expected that. "For suspecting you or catching Rudy Francis?" I asked her with a slight grin, trying my best to ease her angst.

"Definitely the latter," she answered with the whisper of a smile of her own. "I'm not sure how I'm going to live with myself knowing what I did to poor Richie."

"Paige, he knew you were worth the effort. You were one of the reasons he came back."

"Don't say that," she said, clearly in real pain. "That means it's my fault that he's dead."

"I don't see it that way at all," I told her. "Your relationship had nothing to do with why he was murdered. That's all on Rudy, Christy, and their twisted love triangle. Read that letter again once you've had a chance to think about it. He wanted to make things right with you because he loved you as a sister. He wasn't going to give up, and the truth would have come out sooner rather than later. Rudy stole the chance for you two to reconcile, but it was going to happen if he hadn't interfered. That should give you comfort."

"You know what? You're right, it kinda does," she said, the weight starting to lift a little from her shoulders. "Maybe I'm going to be okay after all."

"You will. I'll make sure of it," I said as she stood, and I hugged her fiercely.

I knew that Paige would carry some of the burden of what had happened with her for the rest of her life, but I was going to do everything in my power to ease every bit of it that I could. After all, she was one of my closest friends, and that was what friends were for.

In the end, a man who had disguised himself as Richard Covington's friend had broken the most sacred bond between them and had taken the man's life. He'd pay for it, one way or the other, but it still wouldn't be enough.

I was just happy that the friends I surrounded myself with were true ones, right down to the core.

RECIPES

Apple Cider Donuts

There's something about apple cider that stokes all kinds of good memories for me, and it delights me that I can include the flavor and aroma in donuts, my own special treats. At my house, we all enjoy cold cider, mulled cider, and of course these cider donuts as the weather turns crisp and the light shortens with each passing day. Reducing the cider on the stovetop to intensify its flavor fills the house with magical smells, and this step alone is worth the effort of making these goodies!

INGREDIENTS
 Wet
 1 cup apple cider
 1 cup granulated sugar
 1/4 cup butter, soft
 2 eggs
 1/2 cup buttermilk
 Dry
 4 cups all-purpose flour
 2 teaspoons baking powder
 1 teaspoon baking soda
 1 teaspoon nutmeg
 1 teaspoon cinnamon
 1/2 teaspoon salt

Directions

Preheat enough canola oil to fry the donuts to 370°F.

On the stovetop, heat the apple cider to boiling in a shallow saucepan for 10 to 15 minutes then remove the pan from the heat to cool.

While the cider is reducing, cream the butter and sugar together until they are smooth. Beat the eggs then add them to the mixture, stirring thoroughly.

Next, sift together the flour, baking powder, baking soda, cinnamon, nutmeg, and salt.

Add the dry ingredients to the wet, stirring just enough to blend them all together.

Place the dough on a floured surface and pat out until it's between 1/2 and 1/4 inch thick. Cut out donut shapes or diamonds, or use a ravioli cutter to make round, solid shapes. I always like to include holes as well, as they are a tasty bite-sized treat in and of themselves.

Fry the donuts until they are brown, flipping halfway through the process. This will take 3 to 5 minutes.

Drain the donuts on paper towels then dust with powdered sugar.

Makes approximately 2 dozen donuts.

The Best Homemade Hot Chocolate in the World

Wow, that description sounds like serious bragging, but in our family, at least, it's true! We love to make hot chocolate and enjoy it as a family. If the weather cooperates, we have it by the fire pit outside in the chilly air, and sometimes we even make s'mores to go along with the cocoa. But if it's too cold, too windy, or even too snowy outside, we make hot chocolate and enjoy it in front of a roaring fire in the fireplace, safe and snug inside while the weather outside is frightful indeed!

INGREDIENTS
    2 cups nonfat dry powdered milk
    3⁄4 cup granulated sugar
    1⁄2 cup Hershey's Cocoa, natural unsweetened powder
    1⁄2 cup Special Dark Hershey's Cocoa, Dutch Processed powder
    1⁄2 cup powdered nondairy creamer
    A dash of salt
    Directions
    In a large mixing bowl, combine all of the dry ingredients and mix them well until everything is thoroughly blended. It honestly is as easy as that, though it took me years to get the proportions just perfect!

Store the mix in an airtight container until you're ready to use it. It will last months this way, at least in theory. In our house, it never makes it past two weeks.

When you are ready for hot chocolate, put 1/4 cup of the mix into a mug then add 3/4 cup of hot milk and stir until the powder is dissolved.

Marshmallows are optional.

Makes 8–14 cups, depending on how generous you are with the cocoa mix.

Blueberry Donut Drops

BLUEBERRY IS A FLAVOR that seems to resonate with us in my house. We have always adored blueberry muffins, and one day, I decided to try to replicate the taste and texture of one in a donut form.

As you can see below, I didn't stray far from the basic blueberry mix, but when you've got something that's a winner, why mess with it?

By the way, they also go great with a cup of the hot chocolate listed above.

But then again, what doesn't?

INGREDIENTS

1 package blueberry muffin mix (7 oz.)

3⁄4 cup flour

3⁄4 cup buttermilk

1 egg, beaten

1⁄4 to 1⁄3 cup fresh blueberries (not strictly necessary but delightful as an addition. Frozen blueberries can be used as well.)

Directions

Preheat enough canola oil to fry the donuts to 370°F.

While the oil is coming to temperature, take a medium-sized bowl, add the flour to the powdered muffin mix, and then add the beaten egg and buttermilk.

Stir everything together until the dry ingredients are all absorbed into the liquid, but don't overstir the mix. This is the time to add more blueberries if you so desire.

Drop teaspoon- to tablespoon-sized bits of batter into the oil, using one spoon to scoop up the batter and another one to force it off into the oil.

Turn the donut drops once as they brown then drain on paper towels and add powdered sugar if desired.

Makes between 6 and 10 drop donuts, depending on your portions of batter.

If you enjoy Jessica Beck Mysteries and you would like to be notified when the next book is being released, please visit our website at jessicabeckmysteries.net for valuable information about Jessica's books, and sign up for her new-releases-only mail blast.

Your email address will not be shared, sold, bartered, traded, broadcast, or disclosed in any way. There will be no spam from us, just a friendly reminder when the latest book is being released, and of course, you can drop out at any time.

Other Books by Jessica Beck

Tasty Trials
Baked Books
Cranberry Crimes
Boston Cream Bribes
Cherry Filled Charges
Scary Sweets
Cocoa Crush
Pastry Penalties
Apple Stuffed Alibies
Perjury Proof
Caramel Canvas
Dark Drizzles
Counterfeit Confections
Measured Mayhem
Blended Bribes
Sifted Sentences
Dusted Discoveries
Nasty Knead
Rigged Rising
Donut Despair
Whisked Warnings
Baker's Burden
Battered Bluff
The Hole Truth
The Classic Diner Mysteries
A Chili Death
A Deadly Beef
A Killer Cake
A Baked Ham
A Bad Egg
A Real Pickle
A Burned Biscuit

The Ghost Cat Cozy Mysteries
Ghost Cat: Midnight Paws
Ghost Cat 2: Bid for Midnight
The Cast Iron Cooking Mysteries
Cast Iron Will
Cast Iron Conviction
Cast Iron Alibi
Cast Iron Motive
Cast Iron Suspicion
Nonfiction
The Donut Mysteries Cookbook